Love on the Road

2013

❦

Edited by
Sam Tranum and Lois Kapila

Malinki Press

ISBN 978-0615899039

Copyright © 2013 Malinki Press

For short story writers everywhere who continue, despite it all, to create small worlds in which we can learn about and lose ourselves. Illegitimi non carborundum.

Contents

Foreword

This anthology is the result of a contest we ran from January through March 2013. Writers from the US, Canada, the UK, Ireland, India, Pakistan, Australia, New Zealand, South Africa, and elsewhere submitted stories and we chose our twelve favorites, which we have included in this book.

From among that dozen stories, a panel of judges chose first-, second-, and third-place prize-winners: "L'Amoureux," "Lady in a Tower," and "Cindy in Manhattan." We announced the results in July and sent the authors cash prizes.

We are grateful to judges Anisha Bhaduri, Jennifer Ciotta, Lucas Hunt, Patricia Prizeman, Fiona Spencer Thomas, and Clancy Tucker. We are also grateful to all the writers who submitted stories.

We plan to run the Love on the Road Short Story Contest again in 2014. If you have any questions or would like to enter, feel free to contact us through malinkipress.com. If you like this book, please spread the word about it.

— Sam Tranum and Lois Kapila

L'Amoureux

by

Kathryn Shaver

The lone woman composed her face to what she thought was her best look. Wearing a good suit she had bought the day before in a smart Paris shop, she carried herself in the way a woman does when she wants to be noticed, her posture erect, her chin raised. Late summer sunlight glistened off the water in the round bassin of the Jardin du Luxembourg, though purple clouds menaced the bucolic afternoon in the park. Wishing she might find someone to entertain her for the week she was in Paris, the woman sauntered to the edge of the pool and pretended to watch the small boys scud their toy boats across the water.

The park was dotted with people: squat French-women strolling arm in arm down the esplanade; men resolutely playing boules, the balls clacking against one another; young lovers, limbs entwined, napping on the grass; families with children and dogs and bicycles and skates.

The man she selected was most handsome, tall and slender, of militarily erect posture, and patrician features. She tilted her head and assumed a half-smile. Taking care not to look at him, she flaunted solitary contemplation, signaling her wish for a connection. She danced past the man, then flashed her perfected American smile and moved what she thought was a correct distance away to wait on a bench in the shadow of a stone wall. In a small notebook, she drew a picture of a marionette in the likeness of her most recent lover, its strings controlled by a witch with elongated fingers. His wife, she imagined. She colored the mouth and fingernails black with her pen.

Eugenia Stewart Ellis, a woman of not inconsiderable means, courtesy of her grandmother, was in Paris on her yearly sojourn. This time, once again, she was alone. Her most recent entanglement had been with a man who, as the lovers before him, was less fortunate than she. The romance had ended with a question mark when, only three days before, he had failed to appear at the international departure lounge for a trip to Paris she had given him as a birthday gift. She had left several messages on his phone and, finally, boarded the plane and taken a sleeping pill to erase the

L' Amoureux

image of the empty seat next to her.

Eugenia pretended to concentrate on her drawing as she whispered to herself. *Just for the spite of it, I shall find a handsome lover, take him for mine.* When she allowed herself to look up, the man to whom she had offered her smile stood only a few feet away. The corners of his mouth curled in a disaffected grin that might have been as demonic as it was friendly. He carried a French business newspaper and wore a poplin suit, impeccable, though a closer examination revealed it was frayed.

"*Vous parlez français, madame?*"

"*Oui.*" She drew each vowel long, raising her voice at the end, in her once-excellent boarding school French, which she had somewhat forgotten.

"*Vous êtes Anglaise?*"

No, she wasn't English; she didn't even look English. "*Americaine,*" she answered in a French pronunciation, smiling as she rose from the bench.

He switched comfortably to an inflected English and told her that he was a writer by profession. "Before, I was in business," he said, and explained that he had lost his consulting company a few years before in the French economic crisis of the early 1990s. He was nearly finished writing his book, only a few more weeks, he was certain of it. He presented his personal card, engraved on vellum. Gavril de Chenault. She noted the "de," indicating a family of nobility, and rolled the sound of his elegant name on her tongue.

She introduced herself as Ginna and they began to walk slowly, chatting amiably about the flowers and trees that lined the wide gravel path. He pointed out old-fashioned roses that didn't look at all like roses to Ginna, and a finger-leaved hydrangea with dried crimson blossoms that she told him was quite familiar where she lived. When they reached the massive gates that marked the entrance to the park, he politely pleaded the need to return to work on his book and shook her hand quite formally. On parting, as if an afterthought, he turned and invited her to accompany him to Versailles. Ginna agreed. "*Oui. Demain. Midi.*" Tomorrow at noon. She gave herself time to back out, though she knew she wouldn't. Long ago she had realized, with the aid of a string of psychoanalysts, that she loved the exhilaration of risky romance.

∽

L'Amoureux

Ginna had been to Versailles several times as a tourist, but had never seen it as the handsome Frenchman displayed it. He avoided the interior of the palace, staying outdoors to walk in the late summer pleasantness. First he led her to the Etoile, explaining an architecture of landscape so meticulously planned that the mind and the being are in an enclosure, the eye deceived by a false sense of access to the outside. Ginna looked to where he pointed. His hand, his fingers were elegant, his arm, seductive. She pushed the thought of his physical appeal from her mind and cocked her head to listen, to capture his exact meaning, to please him with her careful attention. From where they stood, at the center of the asterisk, allées of trees led away from them, almost imperceptibly uphill, so that the passages appeared unbound by what he assured her was a wall surrounding the entire star. It appeared that she could take any of five tree-lined paths, all leading to nowhere.

While both Gavril de Chenault and his name were beautiful to her, Ginna discovered a depth of intelligence that captivated her. A horticulturalist by hobby, he named the common and Latin names of every plant and tree. He claimed numerous academic degrees, which he listed for her: Greek, philosophy, and history.

He was writing a book on Catholic theology, he said.

"This terrible life I lead. I have lost everything, my family, my business, my patrimony, all but my book. I have only my book. And my terrible life."

She had rehearsed in her mind all she would tell him of herself. The night before, alone in her hotel room, tingling with anticipation, she had practiced her French, using her inadequate dictionary to remind herself of words she had lost. Speaking to herself in the mirror, she had explained her boarding school life because of her parents' divorce, her marriage at twenty because she was tired of college and could think of no other way to get out of school (finishing had never occurred to her), her divorce at twenty-six, and then the fifteen years of failed romances, a part she elected to omit from the history. But the Frenchman asked little about her, speaking mostly of himself. It disappointed Ginna, as she especially wanted to tell him, to tell someone, of the lover most recently lost.

Finally, "And your faith, *chère* Madame?"

Odd, she noted, that he would want to know her religion and nothing more. Gavril went back to the subject of his book, giving no indication of what he might have thought of her inherited Episcopalianism.

He took her hand and led her past the Grand Trianon into the Petit Trianon, to the make-believe hamlet of Marie Antoinette, stopping to exclaim the beauty of this tree and that — his only friends, he called them — describing in elaborate detail photographs he had taken of each one, at different seasons, in different lights. As they walked across a diagonal forest path, he explained that an unusual weather form had taken the trees down in one spot only. A tornado. It was there where there was no one, in the clearing of a spot nature had destroyed, that he kissed her. Then he took his arms from around her and stepped back, a movement she sensed as timidity, perhaps even embarrassment, on his part, though the embrace and kiss had been of decided deliberation.

"Are you afraid?" he asked, recovering his confidence as unpredictably as he had lost it.

Eugenia was puzzled by his mercurial shift, a flickering glimpse of someone who wasn't what he had been only a moment before. "Should I be, Gavril?"

He didn't answer.

༺༻

For the rest of that week they met daily: at the Chinese porcelains in the Louvre, in a pouring rain in the little garden outside the church of Saint Severin, and finally on the Champs de Mars, gazing up at the Eiffel Tower, as they licked at cones of cassis sorbet. Each day they stopped in a different bistro, sitting squashed among the gibbering French on little chairs on the sidewalk. Over coffee, they had long conversations, switching from English to French and back. Ginna was finally allowed to tell about her own life, painting a picture of a mildly idiosyncratic woman who occasionally smoked cigars, loved jewelry in the shape of insects, and had once had a laboratory rat for a pet. Before parting, she would beg Gavril for the small morsel of chocolate that came with each coffee and he would playfully withhold his until it was time to leave, depositing it onto her saucer when she wasn't looking.

As the days progressed, Ginna realized that perhaps she did have reason to be afraid. Or if not exactly afraid, more perturbed by his eccentricities. Sometimes Gavril spoke not to her at all, but to some outside force, spilling out his anger and frustration at the disappointments of his business and personal life. He spoke repeatedly of unexplained familial violence, of his exile, of his complete aloneness. Once, when

L' Amoureux

they were walking in a park, laughing and punching affectionately at one another in a charade of mock antagonism, she saw a diabolical look cross his face. It frightened Ginna. Not for that moment, not for what might have happened at exactly that instant, but for what might be lurking beneath his surface. It was something she couldn't touch.

On the night before Ginna was to leave Paris, she phoned Gavril late in the evening for a last walk. They strolled arm in arm among trees dripping with the rains that promised autumn, across the Parc des Invalides. Meandering through pools of gentle light from the streetlamps, Ginna could discern lovers in private embrace against shadowed walls. She wanted to be one of those, in a darkened corner, pressed urgently and passionately into lovemaking. While Gavril had kissed her, quite romantically, a few times over these days, she wanted more, expected more. And now, her time in Paris at an end, she was melancholy that her new romance was incomplete.

"Come back with me, Gavril, to my hotel. I don't want this loveliness to end, not just yet."

"As you wish." He complied, with no expression on his face.

They made their way to the sidewalk just outside

of her hotel, where they lingered behind an immense pot of corkscrew topiary. His mood lighter, he insisted they would have to sneak past the night desk clerk to her room.

"The Arab," Gavril said, making a face of distaste, "the Arab must not know." Ginna couldn't imagine why it might be any of the clerk's business or why he even might care. But she went along with the game, feeling a little silly, but also quite young.

As planned, Ginna detained the clerk with questions she had already asked about departure procedures and airport transportation. Gavril slipped quietly by, up the carpeted old steps two floors, to wait at the door of room twenty-three. Ginna took the tiny elevator, which she thought groaned and creaked like a very infirm person trying to stand up. As the lift slowly ascended, Ginna caught a glimpse of her face in the spotted mirror. She was flushed with excitement. She felt tingly and alive with anticipation.

But he disappointed her. A man of Gavril's apparent excellent physical condition should be capable of an erotic performance satisfying to them both. Not only was he unable to consummate their liaison, as a lover Gavril was timid and naïve. Odd, she thought, for a man of his maturity. Yet he spent hours in lavish kisses, probing and penetrating her mouth. She loved the way he held her, how he clutched her as if she might disappear, every part of him touching every part of her.

As a gift for her departure, he had brought her a chapter of his book, which he described as a lexicon of religious thoughts, for those Catholic and not. The chapter he gave her, "*Femme-Homme et Homme-Femme*," made little sense to her. Woman and man, man and woman, against each other, the text said. And then a lot of unconnected sentences about God and Creation that she couldn't understand. Odd scribblings, she thought, as she struggled translating the French.

As she returned to the United States, flying away from him, Ginna tucked the pages of his chapter into the seat pocket in front of her, where she knew they would remain. She sensed in herself a feeling of exhilarated escape. Though she hadn't felt enough danger to run away, the thrill of peril, and of her survival of whatever the risk might have been, coursed through her. She was glad to be leaving him, yet she felt tenderness for him. Dreamily indulging herself, she memorized the moments of their time together, tasting them, trying them out in her imagination, improving the little things that had been not quite right. She surprised herself, feeling emotional — unaccountably so, she thought — about this man who had led her on long walks as he talked and talked and talked. She remembered her amazement at his astonishing knowledge of trees and plants, calling each species of rose by name, of his command of history and literature and language. As for herself, she had said little, and she realized that Gavril hardly knew who she was. But the thought of his lovely hands, his beautiful elegant fingers and how he would touch her arm or her face, warmed her.

Within only days, she received a letter.

Dearest Madame,

This morning I went for jogging in Versailles, in the same way as we walked ... the first time, the Monday after you left ... I saw the sun raising just over the trees behind the marvellous Grand Trianon. It was 8H10 and there were nobody except invisible presences. And you too, dear friend. You brought me something new and very important in my life; so close to me in so many fields! Be sure and confident upon yourself,

L' Amoureux

because I am about you.

> *Dearest one, the last hours were excellent,*
> *Gavril de Chenault*

He signed it in ink, a strong signature, decisively underlined. The letters began to arrive every day, sometimes three in a day, each more passionate than the ones before, tempting her to return.

Très chère Madame,

> *All along the day, hundreds of times, I say "hello, ma petite!" or another expression of tenderness. And I give thanks to the One who conducted your way for a dancing and smiling walk around my seat in the Jardin du Luxembourg. Yes, since that moment, my terrible and marvellous hidden life had changed so quickly, so deeply, so straightly, so nearly to mine, I am flying too, like you, and so grateful.*
> *Gavril*

Ma petite (it is so affectionate in my mouth!),

> *It was … it is … so terrible a time. For a part because of you, but in a good sense. As*

a result, I made several changes to my strange book, all important and very sharp. And also, I am going ahead, stronger, more alive ... (euh! euh! ...) For you, you found into me what you have been searching, since a long time. You found treasures inside me, and a complete solitude and lack of so many... So ... I needed friendship and to be listened and to share what we have to share for human (and divine) living. I was ... and I am ... so glad of our meetings and marvellous time together. Perhaps the first time in my life of such a proximity in so many fields, so peaceful, so equal.

You are sleeping now, and I watch over you very carefully. My love is here and even when she is asleep, our hearts are heart to heart. Remember, my darling, I perceive all you do or is done to your heart, for joy or mutual pain. Keep your way on real peace and joy for our both mutual hearts.

I kiss you like you need, tenderly, "les yeux dans les yeux,"

G.

L'Amoureux

Les yeux dans les yeux. Eyes in eyes. Yes, she needed that gaze, that long, affectionate look. No one on the horizon besides the patrician Gavril de Chenault.

And so she decided to return to Paris.

℘

He had asked her to stay in his tiny garret, flowered in old red paper, with a solitary window that looked out upon the broken panes of abandoned attics and tile roofs across which scampered an occasional rat. As a gift, she had selected a set of the finest knives, Henckels, her idea of lavish practicality for a man who was poor and made all his meals for himself.

Welcoming her, Gavril seemed strange. *"Allo, madame,"* he greeted her. He retained his magnificent French commando bearing, but he was nervous, as if he feared something. He asked if she had received his most recent letter. She had not.

The first evening he made dinner for them. An avocado, cut clean in half with one of the new knives, some breaded fish from a package, heated in a tiny countertop oven, a loaf of fine bread and some cheese. She had brought champagne from the plane, and they drank that, though it was warm.

"What's that pill?" she asked, as they sat on unmatched chairs at a wobbly table. He brushed a small tablet from beside his plate to the floor, turned his head sharply, and began to speak of the economic crisis in France and the resultant unemployment. His eyes were dark.

After dinner, he undressed her slowly, as if for lovemaking. "*Ma petite*," he cooed, untying the scarf that he had chosen for her to buy for herself that afternoon as they wandered down the Rue Saint-Honoré, browsing the exclusive shops. He removed her clothing, folding her shirt, then her trousers and underclothes neatly over the back of a small chair. When she was completely naked, he sat her on the bed and removed his own clothing, putting it away in the armoire piece by piece. Then he cradled her in his arms and fell into a deep sleep. She lay awake, listening to him breathe. Longing for the physicality of his flesh, she chided herself for coming back to Paris for an incomplete liaison. Was this all there was to be? And why? In the middle of the night, Eugenia moved quietly across the room and searched the shelf above the small sink for the identity of the pill Gavril had pushed to the floor. All she could decipher on the prescription bottle was "*anti-psychotique.*"

The next morning, they walked across the Seine on the Pont Alexandre. The gilding of winged creatures atop the bridge glittered in the clear morning sunlight. Ginna caught her breath at the glory of the sight, reminding herself that whatever disappointment she might find in Paris, it wouldn't be in the physical beauty of such a magnificent place. Gavril had begun to talk more than ever, by late in the day, incessantly, sometimes repeating the same phrases again and again, as if finding solace in repetition and rhyme. If she said something to interrupt, he continued on as if he hadn't heard her, as if she weren't there. And while what he said often sounded reasonable and even eloquent, she could make no sense of his elaborate convolutions. His mind expressed a whirling confusion that she couldn't comprehend. When she questioned him in an attempt to understand, he became cross. Then some other thought would enter his brain. His furrowed brow would soften, his irritation would subside as suddenly as it had emerged, and he would look at her affectionately, calling her name in the French way. "*Ma petite, ma petite Eugenie.*"

By the following day, whatever had prevented his amorous success had vanished. Gavril had discarded his sexual timidity. Smiling to himself over his magnificent hardness, he approached her while they were having dinner, in the middle of the night, in the morning, before an afternoon nap, and after. They lay as lovers in the soiled sheets almost incessantly. One day they didn't even dress.

More than once, in the middle of their lovemaking, he rushed to the window and threw it open to inhale great gulps of air, as if there were no oxygen in the room. "Euh. Euh." He didn't even call her name. "This love strangles me." The autumn air was cold and damp, chilling, as she lay naked across the bed. After several minutes, he quieted as suddenly as he had begun to gasp, his torture forgotten, and slept soundly.

As the days passed, he became reluctant to leave his tiny lair, even for food. His diet, unaccompanied by the mealtime pill he had so hastily pushed aside on their first evening, consisted primarily of boiled eggs — which she loathed — yesterday's bread, and apples. She ate practically nothing. She didn't mind, she thought, reminding herself that she was here to be made love to. But after five days, her sexual appetite well satisfied, she wanted more than anything to have dinner in a splendid restaurant. After all, this was Paris.

She chose Le Bourdeille, a small restaurant of the specialties of southwest France. Foie gras sautéed on a salad of frisée greens with a sweet Monbazillac wine. They ate hungrily. Cassoulet, white beans and pieces of pork and goose, prepared in the way of Toulouse, and a fine Merlot. They chatted affectionately, amiably. They ordered coffee and she asked for the bill.

Abruptly, Gavril's face became disturbed. He narrowed his eyebrows and glared at her.

"What is it?" she asked.

"Your face, Satan's face, the face of the rat."

"What? What are you talking about, Gavril?"

"The face of the rat. The rat, the rat, your rat. It's a sign. Your face tells the sign. The face of the rat. Your face tells the sign of the face of the rat."

"I don't understand. We're sitting here having a perfectly pleasant dinner — "

"The name of the rat, your rat, from the devil, a sign. A sign from Satan. A sign, Madame."

Anger overtook her. "A sign of what? Gavril, it was only a pet, a white lab rat somebody gave me when I was in school. It was a long time ago. I named it Mephistopheles, or was it Methuselah, because I thought it was funny and nobody could spell it. I don't even remember telling you about it."

"A sign, Madame, a sign from Satan."

"Are you crazy, Gavril? You're insane."

At the word insane, she saw his face change completely. There flickered a moment of intense hurt, of horror. And then Gavril composed his face. "You, Madame, are a vile serpent. A serpent. A vile serpent." He stood, formally, as if to speak to the room, and then walked out of the restaurant.

The waiter, eyeing her curiously, brought the coffee. Embarrassed, she drank both cups, paid the bill, inquired where she might find a nearby hotel. She walked outside into the cold evening air towards the Champs-Élysées, in the opposite direction from Gavril's apartment, away from this dementia and delusion, away from this madness.

She didn't look back until she heard footsteps just behind her. She was not afraid when she saw it was Gavril, but almost relieved. She wanted to erase the scene in the restaurant, to be folded into his embrace with kisses of forgiveness. He took her arm firmly, in a way that she knew would bruise, and without a word

L' Amoureux

led her back to his garret. Compliant, tears streaming down her face, she yielded to him. She wanted to go back to the sweetness of their romance. Gavril's long legs took the five flights of stairs three at once. Ginna felt she was being dragged up the steps. He pushed her ahead of him into the red room, bolted the door, and put the key on its high shelf.

He took her by both arms and shook her. He shook her so hard that she couldn't speak, only make a guttural sound in her throat. And then he stopped, pushing her away from him. He turned his back to her, went to the tiny window, and leaned his body out into the darkness, sucking noisily, dragging immense gulps of air into himself.

She wailed with great heaving sobs. "How dare you treat me like this. You have no right. I don't deserve it, I don't."

When he didn't turn around, when he didn't even acknowledge her pain, her hurt and disappointment exploded into anger. She spit at his back. It was the ugliest thing she could think to do. She spit again. She flailed her arms at him, ripped his shirt, pushed him. She was small and he was not. Even her adrenalin could not move this tall, strong man who remained with his back to her, filling all the space to the small dormer window, gasping for air, as if begging Paris for all of its oxygen.

She knew she was out of control. Irrational, completely. She didn't care. It felt good. She pulled the books from the shelves of his lone bookcase and threw them onto the floor. She ripped the cover and sheets off the bed and wadded them into a corner. With her arm, she brushed the luncheon dishes from the table as far as she could fling them.

And then she saw the knife. She didn't pick it up, but gazed, detached, at its shiny sharpness, as if it were a museum object. A forgotten image of spilled blood crossed before her: a deer she had hit with her car, years before, its splendid carcass spoiled and awful against the windshield. She wondered if she would take the knife, and if so, what she would do with it. What is it about death that seems such a perfect resolution to an imperfect situation? Her body was motionless.

Gavril's breathing had quieted now, as had she, in horror of her behavior. He turned, looked at her with no emotion whatsoever, and went to the small sink for water. He drank until the glass was empty, refilled it, and handed it to Ginna. Then he undressed for bed, removing his clothes as if he were alone, putting on knitted pajamas with feet in them and a long-sleeved shirt. He pulled the coverlet from the floor and spread it neatly across the bed.

Ginna stood, numb, holding the still-full glass of water. Gavril took the glass from her, set it on the table, and undressed her as if she were a child, not his child, but a child he didn't know. He put his own shirt on her, the one he had worn to the restaurant, buttoned it, and, cautiously taking her by both arms, guided her to the bed.

He lay beside her and slept. All night, he held her closely, his arms around her, as she whimpered. She woke several times, in her sleepy haze, remembering how her father, before he had left home, had held her when she was frightened. That, to Ginna, was what it was supposed to feel like when one is loved. But as she would emerge from the obscurity of sleep, each time she wondered if Gavril was holding her, not from affection, but from his own fear.

In the morning, when both of them were awake, they sat silently for a long time at the edge of the bed. They didn't touch; they didn't speak. Then she telephoned the airlines to find a plane out of Paris that day. He boiled an egg for breakfast and took his pill.

When Eugenia returned home, awaiting her was the letter Gavril had inquired about on her arrival in Paris.

My darling,

If you are shy, I am too. And there are so many reasons not to tell the real truth, I am feeling but I don't know clearly. The most formidable misunderstandings come not from words, but from absolutely different perspectives, of ways of thinking about life and living. Is there no communication and life outside of interior emotions? If you choose to come to Paris, all difficulties will not be lifted.

For way of explaining, a diagnosis when I was nineteen. A car accident, unconscious for two months. My family, my hated family, blaming me for … And then years of electroshock. The way shall be long and difficult if you continue. You lead me indirectly to very serious questions.

I have always kept my engagements and I have never met anyone to go completely to the end of his. Perhaps you were the first. If you

L' Amoureux

choose to come not to Paris, I shall understand.
   Gavril

She never answered the letter.

୧୬

Ginna had always loved Paris. Even so, though
what had been with Gavril was no longer, she was
unable to bring herself to return. She found other
places to travel, other lovers. One summer it was a
painting workshop in Prague, another, a trip to Poland
to tramp with a friend across the overgrown Jewish
cemetery to find his lost ancestors. She drove with a
childhood schoolmate through Spain, from Barcelona
across unbelievable landscapes to Madrid, and took a
package tour of China that she hated.

It was not until several years later, feeling
independent of her emotional attachment to Gavril,
that Ginna decided to return to Paris. Once there,
she felt very alone. She sat on a bench in a tiny green
park at the edge of the Pont Alexandre and gazed at
the triumphant winged steeds atop each column,
remembering how Gavril had led her to that bridge

to see those glittering creatures on a day of brilliant sunshine. She catalogued in her mind the museums they had visited, the parks they had meandered, each bridge they had crossed and re-crossed. The vision of Paris from Gavril's perspective was like no other. Courageous, Ginna dialed the telephone number she still remembered, hoping for the pleasant side of Gavril's voice. "*Allo … oui*," he answered. She was glad for it. Timidly, they agreed to have lunch the next day.

He was as handsome and dignified as he had been that first day she had seen him at the Jardin du Luxembourg, though when he smiled, she could see he had lost a tooth. He carried a newspaper and wore the same poplin suit. He looked wonderful, she thought, startled by the sense of excitement that ran over her body. He kissed her politely on each cheek, then said that he hoped to finish his book soon.

They sauntered along the sandy gardens of the Palais Royal, probed the arcaded gallery of quirky shops filled with military decorations, antiques and curios. They stopped at the window of a stationer who painted family crests. Gavril pointed angrily to the Chenault crest displayed in the window. He explained that the crest had been usurped by his younger brother. "Only the eldest son may take claim to it. And my family pretends I don't exist. So my hated brother has taken it. *Voilà. Gavril n'existe pas.* Gavril. Does. Not. Exist. I don't care. I don't mind. They can't hurt me in my terrible life. I don't care. I don't mind."

The leaves had fallen from the avenue of trees. It was her favorite season to be in Paris, as she could see the architecture. They chose a quiet little restaurant with a view of the long colonnade across the park. "Are you sure, Madame? *It's très cher. Cher. Cher. Cher.* Ex … penn … seef. And I have no money. As you know. I have no money. As you know."

She assured him she had enough money. She insisted. They dined peaceably, though when she reached across the table to touch his arm, he withdrew, as if her touch might poison him. He spoke only of his book.

"My book is completely new. I thought before it was the end. But now I am very close to the end, surely, but it's not the end. Not yet. Something is not clear. So I am working, just in the middle, in the center. Something is not clear and not straight, not linked to action. I work. I work. To clarify. To clarify. To simplify. To simplify. *Voilà.*"

When the waiter brought coffee, Gavril took the

small piece of chocolate from beside his cup and laid it gently onto her saucer. The corners of his mouth turned up in an odd way. He smiled a self-absorbed smile, the same, she remembered, when she had looked up at him from the bench that very first day in the Jardin du Luxembourg.

In perfectly rehearsed French, she told him that she had received his letter, "the one you sent before I came to Paris to be with you the second time. The one I didn't receive until too late. I'm sorry. I'm very sorry, Gavril. I didn't know. I didn't understand your illness. And I didn't understand the drugs that were controlling it. Thank you for your courage in trying to tell me. I understand now."

She looked at her lap and bit her lip. "I'll never understand what happened to me, though." It was her way of apology.

Gavril gave not a flicker of response, as if she spoke in a language he did not understand. They looked vacantly into each other's eyes, two strangers who knew nothing, and yet so very much, about one another.

"*Voilà*," Gavril sang. "*Voilà*." He filled the silence. But he had nothing to say.

After lunch, she walked alone, across the Seine,

towards the Champs de Mars. She bought a cone of cassis sorbet and gazed at the Eiffel Tower. She wondered if she might find someone to entertain her while she was in Paris.

Lady in a Tower
by
Tara Isabella Burton

Roland had no home. He had hostel-beds in London and the seedier districts of Rome; he knew the names of bartenders in Copenhagen and the night bus schedule from Vienna to Berlin. He collected icons in the Balkans; in Trieste, he gave up showering altogether and took to bathing in the sea. He carried with him an antique steamer trunk he'd haggled into thrift in the Marche-aux-Puces. He could barely lift it, but it carried his books, and so he stumbled bravely through melancholy capitals and wind-whistling villages, looking for a place to set it down forever. He slept in railway cars and dreamed of Constantinople.

But Constantinople did not exist, and everywhere else disappointed him. He spent a few weeks in Rome, after university, because he'd read about Falernian wine, and dead emperors, and because he believed that Italian hot-bloodedness could bring him out of himself, and make him forget the books he had read, and make him forget the Rome he had already known. Instead, he paid too much for a room in an apartment near the Campo dei Fiori, an ostensible two-bedroom shared by ten, where the living room smelled of marijuana smoke and the taps did not work, and the sound of Fabrizio's bass drum kept him awake until dawn. He spent a month in Vienna, teaching nasal English to children who laughed at him behind his back; he could not afford whipped cream and velvet-curtained cafes, but wolfed down sausages in the street and walked the graffiti-lined embankments along the Danube.

He continued east, because beauty eluded him. He took night-trains to cities he had never heard of; he fell in love with Albanian waitresses; he could not stop moving. He read Richard Burton by the light of his cell phone in a hostel dormitory in Antalya and believed that, one border-crossing beyond the boundaries of his imagination, he would find that half-dreamed city, with four gates and gleaming towers, that would welcome him at last.

He crossed the plains of Anatolia, and vomited cheap beer into the Black Sea, and when he could go no further he stopped in Tbilisi.

Tbilisi was where everything ended. Visas to

Azerbaijan were prohibitively expensive; to go north to Russia was impossible. The bars on Akhlevediani Street, which everybody still called Perovskaya, were cramped with men like him: English teachers who could not afford flights back home, aid workers who spent their weekdays questioning refugees about their macaroni consumption, journalists with Georgian wives who fattened them on a diet of soft cheese, and who very rarely worked. They got into brawls with locals and altercations with prostitutes; they smoked cigarettes in courtyards and ignored the crowing of chickens. Roland found a splintering and mold-crawling apartment in the old town for a few hundred dollars a month; he bought antique swords from the flea market and lit candles when the electricity went out.

He taught English; he discovered *chacha*, Georgian moonshine, and spent his lessons nursing headaches and picking at the purple bruises underneath his eyes.

But he lived in the shadow of the old fortress, and he inhaled incense at the Armenian church, and he took his yellowing copy of Pilgrimage to Mecca with him to the Azeri bathhouse two Sundays in a row, and imagined that a concubine would appear in the archway of his cabin, with hair down to her toes and jasmine pinned to her robe, with unintelligible poetry on her lips, and promise him a homecoming.

The masseuse was sixty, naked, and fat; her breasts slapped against him while she kneaded his shoulders. Roland dropped the Burton in the bath; even when it dried, five days later, it still smelled strongly of sulfur, and he had no choice but to throw it out. He punched a wall; he packed his steamer trunk. He realized there was nowhere left to go.

Then he heard about the woman in the tower.

Roland got the information in the customary Georgian way — from one of the sellers of tiger-skins in the flea-market, who offered him moonshine and made him stroke the eviscerated head. Winter was coming, he said, in a mongrel, tongue-tripping conglomeration of Russian, Georgian, and English, and the tourists and the villagers were making their way down from the mountains.

But the ambassador's wife had refused to leave. She had sent him back to Tbilisi without her. There had been an incident — the skin-seller could not say what. She had sat down in the ruins of one of the crumbling stone towers in Mutso, unpacked her suitcase, and declared that she was staying. She'd sent for her things

Tara Isabella Burton   33

— it had taken a whole *marshrutka* to carry her books up the pass — and slept beneath the stars.

"Crazy!" The skin-seller laughed, and the lolling head of the tiger laughed with him. "Crazy woman!"

The ambassador had denied all this, of course — Violet Sandhurst had simply caught a cold, he said; she'd be returning within the week — but the driver who'd ferried the books had told Dato's third cousin the truth. She was mad; it was impossible; the roads would soon close. She would run out of food; after the first snow, even the helicopters would not be able to reach her.

Roland's heart began to ricochet around his chest, and in the thrill of the moment he closed his eyes and saw how it had been with her. She had gone to the mountains; she had seen in the stars and the ridges and the wailing emptiness of the mountaintop something great and glorious, and something almost like home. The rivers had welcomed her; she had heard in the cricket-song the melody she had been humming under her breath her whole life without knowing it. She had felt her hands against the tower-stone and known that, at last, there was a place in the world where she belonged.

Roland's vision blurred and went double, and she was the only thing he saw clearly: traced upon the stars, treading on mountaintops, filling her crumbling tower with antique swords and holy icons, crying in unintelligible tongues the magic spells that evoked the spirits of the dead from the crypts at Anatori, and awakened the demons from the horned altars that lined the mountain path.

He left the next morning for Mutso. He sat seven hours in a *marshrutka*, with a sack of potatoes for a pillow, next to a fish-faced Armenian woman who insisted on feeding him lemon-flavoured crisps until he was sick.

In splintering Russian, the driver told him that the last *marshrutka* back was tomorrow; it would be the last one of the season. If he wanted to stay longer — the driver snorted at the idea; there was nothing to see in Mutso — he would have to walk back to Tbilisi himself.

The *marshrutka* puttered off; everything was still.

The mountains floored him; their emptiness coursed through him. If he stretched his neck he could just make out the village at its peak: a sprawling and Gothic conglomeration of stone. The path was empty; moss and vines choked the life out of anthills. A few iridescent beetles slipped in and out of the rock. Roland laughed, and his laughter came back to him, refracted into echoes, and the shiver of his spine sent him reeling, and the earth seemed to rumble with the beating of his heart.

It was the first thing that had not failed him in ten years.

He lugged the steamer trunk up the mountain; it took him two hours and the effort made his fingers bleed. The sight of the blood filled him with wild joy, and he crowed aloud when at last he had slumped and scrambled over the final outcropping of rock, and the whole world lay green and dark and boiling with life beneath him.

She was sitting by the ruins of a chapel, with mud on her shoes and her fingers twisted in her lap. Her hair was long and red and braided, and although her head was not crowned with flowers, Roland knew that it should have been.

In his heart he knew she had been waiting for him.

"Has he sent you to bring me back?" Her smile was grim and she did not look at him. "Because I won't go back — you're wasting your time. And his."

"Nobody's sent me," said Roland.

"But you're not a tourist." She leaned back, cat-like, on the rock, and surveyed him along with the rest of her kingdom. "It's September."

Lady in a Tower

"I'm not a tourist," said Roland.

"Then what?"

The wind whistled around them; the buzzing of the beetles deafened them. Roland searched himself and found he had no reason to lie to her. "I heard about your tower," said Roland. "I came to see if it was true."

"Of course it's true," she said, with a sharpness that chilled him.

"Then you're Mrs. Sandhurst?"

"I am," she laughed softly and stood. "And this is my tower." She pointed to the tallest of the remaining battlements, a freestanding pile of stone through whose cracks he could make out the other side of the mountain. The lower part of it was weathered; Roland could make out where the rebuilding had begun, where a few precarious slabs of brick had been plastered over what remained of the old fortress.

"And you live here?"

"There's a generator." She did not look at him. "And I've got food."

"You're not cold?"

She flinched. "I've got what I need. I had them drive a van up, all the way from Tbilisi. With everything I needed."

She took him to the tower and took away the plank of wood from the doorway. "You see, I've brought it all."

When Roland saw the tower he knew that he had come home.

Books were piled into approximations of furniture — she had made them into chairs with high backs, and into a serviceable dining table, and even into a bed, for she had thrown four or five sheepskins over a series of hardbacks in one of the corners of the room.

"It'll be dark soon."

He held out his hand; he opened his palm and offered her matches.

"I brought them for you," he said. "I thought you might need some more."

"What's this?" she said. "I have enough."

He stammered and his ears turned pink. "I thought — just in case."

"I don't need any help," she said. He looked down and she softened. "What is it that you want, then?"

He opened his mouth; he closed it again. He tried to make sense of it — of her — of the glorious unreality of her red hair and her tower made of books, of the ricocheting echoes of the mountainside. There were icons on the shelves and the bed was made of books.

There were Karabakh carpets along the walls and the tower smelled of candle-wax. There were no empty beer-bottles, no vomit stains, no piles of dirty laundry. There was nothing but an altar she had repurposed — yes, it was an altar! — dangling the customary horns from a nail she'd driven into the wall, nothing but books, nothing but beautiful things.

"I have nowhere else to go," he said.

She knelt down; she peered at him. She took his face between her hands and stared at him until his throat went dry from fear.

"Do you want to stay here?" Her voice trembled slightly. "Is that it?"

Roland sank to his knees and breathed in the smell of dust and of wildflowers, and set down his steamer trunk at her feet.

"I want to stay here," he whispered.

He half-expected her to laugh; she did not laugh. She did not mock him; she did not throw his trunk and all his household goods over the edge of the mountainside.

He could not stand it; he kissed her. He pulled her into him and wagered everything he was or ever had been on the possibility of that kiss, on its ability to transmit to her in the space of lip upon lip that he understood everything about her, about her tower, about her books, and that it floored him.

She stopped him; she pushed him away. For a moment everything shattered.

"You're awfully forward, aren't you?" She looked at him, deliberating with cat-eyes.

He scrambled for an apology, but her smile silenced him.

He looked into her eyes and saw them darken.

It was not real, and yet nothing was real. Reality had left him with the stench of the *marshrutka*, with his sweat-sogged sheets, with the oily puddles that leaked from his kitchen sink. Everything that made sense, everything that tethered him to the cities that did not shine when he passed through them, and to Constantinople which was not Constantinople, had vanished. She was not real — she could not be real — he had conjured her, out of his loneliness, out of books he had read and lives he had not lived.

Nothing else was real.

He made love to her the way Sir Richard Burton would have made love to a concubine, and the weight of her in his arms brought the planets into orbit. He tucked the condom wrapper underneath the carpet and brushed her hair from her shoulders. He unlatched his steamer trunk; he unpacked his books while she dozed.

Afterwards, the stars came out, and Violet stared out at them through the holes in the ceiling.

"It's driving him mad, you know," she said. "That I'm here."

He kissed her breasts; he had come home.

"I won't go back either," he said. "Not ever. No more horrid beer. No more piss-stained underpasses. No more lesson-plans — "

"Is that what you do?" She stretched out across the sheepskin. "I did wonder." She laughed softly to herself and did not wait for an answer. "One hundred thousand lari," she said. "That's how much I've spent on this place." She yawned and rolled into him. "That's how much of his money I've spent on this place. But he can't stop me."

Roland did not hear her. He was too busy counting the stars, bathing his face in moonshine. He read the spines of the books and greeted them like old friends; he traced his fingers along the ones that served them now as a bed, awash with gratitude, shuddering with joy.

"Have you read them all already?" He thought he

could make out Pilgrimage to Mecca among them in the candlelight; he could no longer breathe.

"Read them?" Her laugh punctured the air. "God, no. They're Edward's." She had put her clothes back on.

"Edward's?"

"He loves them. All he does is sit in that ridiculous armchair of his and snivel over them! He's afraid to even read them — he's afraid he'll damage them!" Her lips curled at the edges. "Not anymore, of course. The damp's gotten to them already." She threw her head back and laughed. "He was furious, you know. When he found out."

Sense barreled back into him; Roland spluttered and sat upright. "What do you mean?"

"Don't worry," she said. "It's completely legal. They're half mine, after all. And he does deserve it."

"Why?"

"Why do you think?" she snapped. "In any case, it doesn't matter." She passed her eyes over Roland's nakedness. "We're even now, he and I."

"And the carpets?"

"He'll have a hell of a time trying to get them down." She lit a cigarette; the air choked him and he began to cough uncontrollably.

"And the tower?"

The stars had fallen from their constellations; they shot into the earth and flamed out. Nothing made sense; everything made sense.

"He really thinks I'll stay this time," Violet continued staring out over the mountainside. "You know, I nearly did, once. When we were in Bosnia. We had gone for a few weeks to a cottage in Montenegro for the summer. Found the texts he'd sent this attaché at the embassy — it wasn't the first time, either. Well, I threw a fit and told him I wasn't moving from that cottage — not ever! And I stayed, too. For a week! Until he'd made a damn fool of himself trying to lure me back to Sarajevo."

"Why did you go back?"

She shrugged. "Why not?"

"Then you will go back?"

For a moment she fell silent. She looked at him and swallowed and she flushed slightly when she spoke. "The last *marshrutka*'s tomorrow," she said. "The last for the whole season. I haven't got a choice."

He stumbled over syllables and found that there was nothing he could say.

When she spoke again her voice was harsh and

she avoided his gaze. "The generator's solar-powered, you know. It'll be useless once the snow starts. But… ," She sighed and waved him away. "But he'll have to bring the books back himself." Her laugh rattled in her throat. "It's always the same with him."

Roland did not look at her.

"You do understand, don't you?" She put her hand on his and gripped it.

He nodded.

"You'll want a space in the *marshrutka*, won't you?"

"Probably," he said.

In the morning they went down together, and sat next to the Armenian, who had by now exhausted her bag of lemon-crisps. They got a flat tire at Roshka; the journey took twelve hours and the *marshrutka* smelled of stale carrots and to pass the time they talked about the weather. When they returned to Tbilisi they kissed one another on the cheek and then awkwardly shook hands; he took the Metro home to his flat in Sololaki, where the power had gone out. In the dark he packed and repacked his steamer trunk, and in the morning he took the bus to Istanbul.

Cindy in Manhattan

by

Kimberly Cawthon

Today, Rob will unlock a safety deposit box that will reveal the secret decade of his mother's life. Cindy was thirty-one when he was born and, like Jesus' mysterious eighteen-year trek off the biblical grid, Rob doesn't know what happened from Cindy's nineteenth birthday until her thirty-first.

Our past Manhattan adventures were in pursuit of pizza, beer, Broadway and people watching, but today, on this sticky Thursday in July, we're on Rob's mission.

We descend wet concrete steps, down, down, down, through loops and people movers. The loud screeches and whooshes of passing metro cars drown out Rob's cursing when he realizes the ticket machine won't accept his nickels.

"Who doesn't accept friggin' nickels? This is America!" Rob pounds the buttons and I watch his teeth bite and pull back his bottom lip as he prepares to unleash a tirade of the word, fuck — a word so embraced in this part of the country, it's practically punctuation.

"Why did you bring those? That's our Vegas buffet money," I scream against the noise of the subway station.

He ignores me and continues to pop nickels in the slot only to hear them immediately bounce out the tiny metal square reserved for pennies and gold dollar coins etched with Sacagawea's face and baby. Robert's brazen Jersey accent thickens with every word and new level of annoyance.

"Try some of my nickels. They're less bossy." I laugh, hoping to see Rob smile, but he doesn't. His rushed scowl doesn't budge. I twist open the coin purse of the giraffe-print wallet I've had since seventh grade.

"Forget it," Rob snaps and shoves in a crisp twenty-dollar bill.

I forget how impatient Rob becomes when we're in his town. Rob was born in Manhattan, raised in Jersey and reared on subways, delis, and attitude. This is his home and I realize that even at my quickest, I'm too slow for Rob. He never used to mind my pace but today he's a snippy ball of stress.

The subway car isn't too crowded. Rob and I find two open seats and sit beside each other. It smells of

French-fry grease and city grime unique to New York. I've smelled similar grimes — in a Paris taxi, in a London phone booth — but New York has its own breed of gross. It's metallic like a mechanic's garage and garlicky from kebab, hotdog, falafel and curry vendors sputtering salty balls of scent into the hot smog of carbon dioxide and excess. Oh, and one can't forget the lingering stink of street garbage that combines all smells into a fermenting bag of death so foul, the thought of it makes me light-headed. Yet, even at its smelliest, I think this town is one of the greatest cities our little blue planet has to offer.

"Do you remember when we were here for New Year's and we had to step over that passed-out bum covered in barf?"

He nods but doesn't look at me. Rob is too distracted. He's wondering if his mother was an escort in Rome or whether she was a mercenary for some rebel political group or maybe she shacked up with a Greek cheese-maker and popped out a few half-brothers and sisters Rob never knew about. Cindy died last March — a heart attack over St. Patrick's Day weekend at her favorite Jungle Wild slot machine in Atlantic City. Rob got a load of old jewelry, his grandmother's bone china stolen back from the Nazis, a timeshare in Key West and two storage units filled with furniture, mementos, and other crap from Cindy's beloved Sedona, Arizona. He didn't want anything but the key — the key to that box, a key opening forty years into her past.

My stomach growled.

"Can we eat before we go to the bank?" I ask.

He gives me a disappointed look.

"I'm starving," I say, holding a hand over my stomach. "I haven't eaten anything since the plane peanuts this morning."

Rob nods. He's quiet and deep in thought. His hand hasn't left the pocket of his jeans; his fist holds the key in a vice grip.

The subway stops. We disembark into a crowd of multi-tasking commuters — all ears plugged with headphones or cell phones. As we ride the escalator up to the surface, Rob briefs me on the path ahead.

"Do not look up. You always look up and then I lose you. Stay behind me. Look straight ahead and keep walking."

"What if we get separated?"

"Keep walking. Go into a shop and ask for Angelo's and I'll meet you there. Don't look up." He points a stern finger at me.

Rob is right to tell me this. I can't help it. The buildings stretch up forever. I'm from a land where the sky never ends, but here it is obsolete. It's all metal, glass and shadow ascending higher and higher as my neck dips further and further back. I'm in awe of how small the city makes me feel. The last time I was so captivated, an existential trance soon followed — my steps slowed, my focus drifted — Rob disappeared into the crowd and when he doubled back to find me, there was a thief's hand in my pocket, another one on my purse and I was staring up, oblivious to it all. As we walked to Times Square those many Decembers ago, I was nearly mugged while taking a picture of the Empire State Building, which grabbed my eyes with its red and green Christmas flare.

"I don't look up all the time," I say.

Rob scoffs.

I do my best to keep my skyward gazes minimal. I grab Rob's hand and shuffle behind him as he expertly maneuvers and plows through the crowded sidewalks. We bob and scoot for a few blocks until we make a sharp right turn into a tiny door. We're in a tight line of people. Rob slides me in front of him so I can read the menu. I breathe in the smell of fresh dough crustifying in their stone ovens. Cheese bubbles. The peppery whiff of basil and marinara swirls its way up our nostrils and I float. Angelo's is crowded with the lunch rush or maybe this is how it always is. It doesn't take us long to move down the line and order a medium half cheese-and-tomato, half bacon-and-jalapeño pie.

We find a table, blue cups of Diet Coke in hand, staring at opposite sides of the room. Rob's foot and hand tap impatiently.

"Can you relax a bit?" I say.

"The bank closes in two hours," he says.

"We'll make it."

The waiter floats the pizza tray over Rob's head and lowers it gently onto our table. The silver circle overflows.

"It's hot folks," the waiter says in a quick dash back to the kitchen.

My half is cheese-and-tomato because I consider myself a pizza purist who doesn't like too much interfering with flavor dissection. Rob loves heat. As a chronic victim of nasal problems and a smoker for ten years plus, his deadened food senses and warped taste buds are only remedied with fire and spice. He surprisingly reaches for a plain slice off my side first. We both grab and fold. Rob bites. His eyes close and he gives the table three hard pounds. I push his soda glass in front of him, knowing he's bit into pizza-lava. He doesn't take it but stays with his eyes closed, chewing slowing; a huge smile breaks across his face.

"Jesus Christ," he mumbles with a mouthful of wet cheese and dough.

"Good?" I say through my own full mouth.

"There should be goddamn symphonies," he chews and swallows and takes in a breath, "written to worship the Jersey tomato."

I laugh and let the delicate, buttery crunch break across my eager tongue.

"Do you think she was a prostitute?" I ask with a smile. He shrugs his shoulders.

"I wanna say no, but I don't know," he says.

"I could see Cindy doing it. High-class. Maybe Vegas. Or even better, the French Riviera. Cindy knows French, right?"

"I think so. At least the curse words."

"That's all one really needs," I smile. "Or maybe Germany? They love blondes who pout. She would have made a mint in the Fatherland — a sexy *shiksa* like her." I wink.

My attempts to bring humor are shot dead. Usually Rob enjoys my attempts at Yiddish but not today.

Rob grabs two slices, lays them on top of each other and hastily vacuums them into his face. He gives me a stern eye and I hear his demand in my head, sweet and forceful — hurry the fuck up. I savor what I can of the pizza and rapidly slurp the soda until I feel my stomach poof out and tiny burps rise up in my throat.

"Robbie. Jeeze. Let me swallow," I say.

"Wow. Saucy," he says with a mischievous expression that took my comment straight to Planet Pervert.

"You pig. Shut up." I can't help but laugh. I'm happy to see Rob snicker with me.

There are moments when I stare at Rob, his funny face, his glasses, his stubble. He's handsome. It is these moments — brief, secret — I wish Rob weren't gay. We've been friends just shy of a decade. He's the longest male relationship I've had. He's seen my face sans eyeliner and gloss, seen me cry, barf, get high, get drunk, have sex in the room next to his. We can fart next to each other and if needed, discuss the oddities and infrequencies of bowel movements. To be Rob's friend is to be free. He is the one person who I have been truly, completely myself with. I've never had to hide my quirks and peccadilloes for fear he would think me ugly or un-cool. There are these odd little moments, perhaps pulled out from my own biology as a woman, where I look at Rob and wonder why we aren't together. It doesn't help that Rob is the straightest gay man I know. He passes for a father of two with a college bride he wooed in Anthropology class. It makes things complicated. They don't last — those moments — they flee like that odd ringing in your ears or a piece of food stuck in your teeth. But still. I don't like them. I don't want to think of Rob that way. I can't. It's too pathetic.

"The cashier was cute, did you see him?" I ask Rob while elevating my eyebrows.

"Eh. He had an overbite."

"That can be fixed. Nice nose. I like."

"No. Post-dental work applicants only."

"What a shallow brat you are."

"Proud of it," Rob says while standing up.

I'm still chewing a warm, crunchy piece of crust as we head for the door. We squeeze through the tiny cracks of space around tables filled with people lifting pizza to their mouths. The city smells hit my face — car exhaust, new plastic, ink. We veer right and plug back into the throngs. Rob is six-foot-three, and keeping his pace is nearly impossible. He holds my wrist and pulls me so my legs move to meet his long strides. I look up to find the sky and trail the height of the buildings. I imagine a television or an antique curio cabinet plummeting down, instantly obliterating us. The thought makes me shudder. I look forward and quicken my pace so we're in step. Faces whirl past me in a blur. I count how many headphones I see, cell phones, designer sunglass bought in a Chinese corner store.

"So you know that expression — how does it go? 'Kicking ass and taking names?'" I ask.

"What?" Rob leans over to hear me.

"You know, 'I'm kicking ass and taking names.'"

"Yeah sure."

"Did that start here?"

"Probably."

"I love that expression, but I don't get it."

"What's not to get?" he says.

The crowds thin out as we cut through a few residential blocks. The brownstones have flower pots along the edges and American flags wave with July pride.

"Why do you need to take names? That's stupid."

"It's just a thing," Rob says, impatience in his voice.

"Okay, you're kicking ass, you're doing good and what — you have a little notepad where you ask for peoples' names?" I say.

"I don't think you're literally jotting down anything."

"Then why do you take names? What's the point of saying that? What are you going to do with the names? Are you supposed to tell those taken names that you kicked ass later on? Or are the peoples' names you're taking the ones whose asses you kicked?"

Rob is quiet for a minute. He makes a swift left and I jerk along like a rag doll. My shoulder pops against the movement. I wait for his answer and take in the change of sound and smell of grass when Rob stops abruptly and breaks our grip to dig around his pockets.

"Shit," Rob mutters as he pulls out the cloth lining of his pockets. I see the fear on his face.

"I can't find the key," he plunges both fists into his back pockets.

"Calm down. You have it."

He feels around the front pocket again and we hear a faint ding of metal hitting sidewalk. The tiny key is millimeters from plummeting down a grate. Rob's gasp is loud and filled with terror. He gently picks up the key and encloses it in a tight fist. All the color has drained from his face.

"Let me put it in my purse," I say.

"No. I need a chain."

Rob's long legs take him in feverish strides down the block. I follow behind him, nearly jogging to keep his pace.

We pass by dozens of mysterious doors, windows overflowing with goods. I walk by a cheesecake bar, a bagel shop, a steakhouse and over fourteen hot dog stands. Though my stomach is filled with pizza, my brain wants to attack every delicious, unique bit of these Manhattan essentials. This city and I only get together once a year, sometimes less, and when we reunite, my appetite is insatiable. I blame the smells.

I eye a dingy bed sheet on the ground covered with designer purse knock-offs. The purse dangling by my side is a fake Dolce & Gabbana I bought from Rob's Turkish ex-stepmother Tulay the year before. Her eyes were the deepest brown, a pigment away from solid black; her house smelled of a thick, musky perfume and greasy meat. I gasped when she pulled out the intricate, black-and-gold, faux-leather lump of artful buckles, loops and zippers from a rumpled trash bag. Tulay claimed the purse "fell off the truck" and could be mine for no less than sixty bucks — the real one cost a semester's tuition. My new purse sat in my lap as we ate thrashed chunks of baby lamb right off the body. The animal lay on a long golden platter, shiny and stoic like a kingly lion. Tulay gave me the eyeball to eat, saying it was good luck; it would make me smart. I sliced the globular ball in half, giving Rob a piece. I chewed the slippery hunk, part snot, part gristle, part plastic. The medicinal bite of the eye fluid nearly sent lamb and rice throttling back up.

"Robe," Tulay said in her Turkish-Jersey flare, "Robe, you should marry diss girl. Gewd match for you."

"Tulay, you know I prefer men." Rob said in between heavy glugs of sangria.

"She does too. See! Lots in common!"

I wished Tulay was Rob's real mom. My Mexican-Catholic grandma, *se llama* Fidelina (whose death cannot come soon enough) would count that comment as speaking ill of the dead — an offense she used to scold me for when any word other than saint was used for the recently departed. I think she was paranoid about curses. *Abuela* Fidelina is a bitch and so was Cindy. Maybe bitches have to worry about curses. Technically, I'm not speaking ill but rather stating facts. Even Rob would agree. A few years ago, I asked him what Cindy thought of me, if the cold hug and half smile were reserved for women who irked her, but Rob assured me she looked at everyone that way — best friends and worst enemies. Cindy was austere, shallow and calculating. I'm pretty sure she hated me, like she hated Tulay, undercooked meat, The Sierra Club, waiting in line, colored contact lenses and anyone — man, woman, child, bird or beast — who, for one-tenth of a second, made her feel stupid.

Rob kneels so I can fasten the chain around his neck. It's silver and sturdy.

"No guido jokes please," he says.

I go for it anyway.

"You sure your name isn't Vinny?" I say.

"Really? Really. After I just said not to?" he huffs.

His stress is morphing into anger. I change the subject.

"Do you think we'll have time to visit Tulay?"

"She's upstate with her new boyfriend, Juice."

"Juice?"

"Yeah, he's Ecuadorian or something."

"What?"

But Rob says nothing more. I watch him tuck the key and chain underneath his shirt and take off down the block, pulling me along to mentally scratch my head. Is he angry with Tulay? I almost need a daily briefing of who Rob is angry with. It changes from hour to hour. I think it's his Greek/Sicilian roots that dole out love and punishment with the same hand. Or it's just Rob — fickle, finicky and vengeful — a child of Cindy's black-and-white tutelage. For example, Rob's father was an accountant on Wall Street who was stabbed to death in a dingy SoHo alley when Rob was a toddler. I was horrified when Rob first told me. I gave my sympathy but he didn't want it, neither did Cindy.

"Eh. It was the 80s," he said. "Plus he was cheating on my mother with some whore from Queens. He got what was coming."

And just like that, a man's memory was shoved into the gutter, only the bad remembered. A part of me hopes Robbie feels more for his slain father than what he outwardly shows but the longer I know him, the less I think that. Cindy's other boyfriends and husbands were fair substitutes, though Rob never mentions them unless he wants to go on a tirade of which ones he hated the most.

There is always a lingering hair of concern that Rob may abruptly cut ties with me should I offend him in some unforgivable way. I've seen him do it. I've seen it happen to other boys and girls who were offended by Robbie's brashness, his impatience. They disappear from his life — those who dogged musicals, who failed to see the supreme holiness of *The Sopranos* — they were pitched like newspaper at the bottom of a birdcage. This is why Rob can't keep a boyfriend for longer than a few months. He looks for the bad, the flaws, the wrong things and dips out before he can remove his armor. I told him this once and he didn't speak to me for a week. I got off light. On the other hand, after all this time, a part of me feels I may be exempt from Robbie's wrath. After the five-year hump of being his friend, I think I reached elite status. I consider myself a VIP. Though Rob and I have fought, ignored each other, gone a few weeks without giving a damn, he's always reeled me back into his corner and I've always happily returned. I don't know how or why but, like Rob says, "Why question a good thing?"

We continue walking, weaving, maneuvering. The smells curl and seep into one awkward, indefinable, scent that lines my nostrils in strangeness.

"When we get home, I think I'm going to try online dating," I say.

"What do you mean try? You were chitchatting with that Cincinnati guy for weeks."

"No. That didn't count. I made a profile with you on that discounted-weekend thing. I wasn't really, truly ready. I think I am now."

"Where did that revelation come from?" he says.

I don't answer him. I don't tell him I've got a bad itch. The itch to flirt. The itch to blush. The itch to have a conversation with a man and have it possibly end up in a dry-hump. It's been almost two years since the li'l missy down south got more than DIY. My last boyfriend/sexual partner was a big drinker. I got tired of picking up his whiskey-soaked ass at 3 a.m. with bar skanks trailing behind his stumbles. For nearly twenty-four months, I've been sobering up from him and others that could be his twin. If I tell Rob about it, he'll advise me to fluff the hair, shorten the skirt and flaunt the goods at the local watering hole, but he doesn't realize the itch wants more than sex. I need to create this kind of bond — this wonderful rhythm and connection within the straight girl/gay man dance — with someone else, someone who will go to that place with me, that place sans make-up, a push-up bra and teeth-whitening, that place of freedom and fearlessness and alcohol maturity. I need another best friend, preferably one who wants to hang out with my vagina.

They do exist, though it's hard to remember when the most important person in your life wouldn't screw you if it meant preventing nuclear fallout. It's a matter of time before a new guy steps in and if I have anything to do with it, the time will come sooner than later. But for now, for today, let it be Robbie and me, corned beef sandwiches, gossip, favorite lyrics from *Les Miserables* — side by side like two old oak trees.

"Do you think she was in prison?" I ask.

We stop moving. Robbie doesn't answer me. He dips his head back to survey the immense building in front of us.

"This is it," he says while pulling out a cigarette.

"Why is there always time for carcinogens?" I say.

"I'm nervous."

I watch Rob smoke his cigarette with shaking fingers. I sit on a ledge, hearing the blaring horns of bumper-to-bumper cabs.

"I was twelve when I first asked her," he said after a drag.

"She told me she was an astronaut. I believed that one for a long time," he shook his head. "I think that was the reason I wanted to go to space camp so badly. I wanted to be like her."

Rob stomps his cigarette and opens the door.

Cindy in Manhattan

"I'm glad it's you and me today," I tell him as we step into the elevator. I try to sound as aloof and nonchalant is possible. Robbie doesn't need to go the deep-friend-zone with me now.

"Of course," he says, with just as much detachment.

The elevator closes and we lift, ascending higher and higher. The elevator is glass. I watch the people shrink, the taxis become the size of Hot Wheels.

"I'm going to get you a cat when we get home," I say.

"Oh shut it, I hate cats," he says.

"No you don't. You forgot you liked them."

"What about a little Weimaraner?" he says. "I love their color."

"No. I'm buying you a cat and its name will be Andrew Lloyd Webber."

Rob bursts into a healthy chuckle. He grabs my hand and entwines our fingers like we're pre-teens at the mall.

"Deal," he says.

It's a stoic waiting room, beige, with chairs potentially recycled from 1977. I sit down and my gaze encircles the clear view of treetops, the tips of skyscrapers — Manhattan in the sky. The security guard behind the desk offers me a glass of water. Rob is the only one who can see the box's contents. I don't push to accompany him. It's for him. He's lead into a locked room. I hear his loud exhale as he walks in.

Moments with Cindy flash before my eyes. Her short, blonde bob, her thin lips. I didn't know the woman well, but what I saw, what I encountered never screamed maternal. I didn't know many mothers who threw twenty-dollar bills at their sons' faces, telling them to get the hell away from the roulette wheel with their bad juju. I didn't know many who abandoned their sons on their fourth birthdays with the families of their Jamaican nannies, only to return nonchalantly on their fifth without explanation or remorse. When Rob came out, there was no support or loving words but rather a shrug of her shoulders and her graveled, smoker's throat saying, "Robert, I don't care if you walk in with a toaster on your dick. It's a phase. It's men now and in a few months it will be something else. Don't label what's bound to change."

A feeling comes over me. It's a cold breeze, a lip shake, a tingling. I know whatever Rob sees in that box will be awful. No offshore accounts stuffed with money, no patents to multi-million dollar inventions, no famous bloodlines — nothing that could be praised in the light, spoken from her mouth. That box is Cindy's shame, shame so immense, so layered, it couldn't be faced until she was worm food. I don't know why Rob or I ever thought it could be positive. Something locked away, something hidden this long is pure poison.

I wait for a long time. I put on lip balm, lotion my hands, brush my hair, tweeze a few stray eyebrow hairs. I sit and stare out at the immense city in the soundless room smelling of an old library. I hear the click of the door. Rob is ghostly white. He takes quiet steps and sits on the chair next to me. The words want to fly from my mouth, the questions; I lock them behind a hard bite and closed lips. He looks down at the floor and then at me. A thick line of sweat slides from his sideburn. I put a delicate hand on his knee. Then the tears. His face contorts into devastation and the most desperate sob begins. I've never seen Rob cry like this before, not even at her funeral. I've never seen tears like these, dripping fast, red face; it's scary to see someone you love break in front of you. I want to slip into the elevator and fall away from it, the moment — dark and unmovable — the realness of life and the stinging handprint across your face.

Rob is suddenly a little boy in my arms, wailing. I let him cry. Years from now or maybe minutes from now, I might break apart this moment. Were Rob's tears from the box or was it the cold, new reality that his mother is truly gone? I'll most likely hear about what that box revealed every day for the next twenty years. I see Rob's brokenness and right then, I don't push him to tell me. I wipe his tears with the end of my sleeve. Rob's shoulders heave, his breath catches. Our hands stack on top of each other's, a tight little wall of support and collapse. On top of the world, in the quiet space where glass and steel marry, I cry with my friend. I say to him, "We'll figure it out Robbie. We'll figure it out."

April in Leningrad

by

Nina Shengold

It is her jacket that catches my eye, a leather too fine to have come from a Soviet cow. Her boots look Italian; her blue jeans, American, but so are everyone's now if they have enough money. Her hips have a Mediterranean sway and her dark hair gleams like a mink pelt, catching the evening sun.

Yes, Italian, I'm sure of it. And she is walking alone, without a husband or boyfriend or even an Intourist guide. I walk faster, hoping to reach her before the light changes. Perhaps a slight brush of the arm, an excuse to apologize, to look into her eyes. I have just this one moment before she will cross Nevsky Prospect and disappear into her foreign hotel. I must speak now or lose her.

Why did I dress in this windbreaker? Only in Russia could such ugly fabric flap over the back of a man, twenty-five, an adult who has already married, divorced and is once again wearing a jacket picked out by his mother. I picture Mama, her flowered scarf knotted below her chin, standing for hours on line in the basement of one of the state stores. This Italian knows nothing of Soviet shopping.

The light blinks. She has stopped at the corner, she waits there for me. I could offer a cigarette if it were Marlboro. I move alongside for a glance at her face. There's enough of a crowd at the curb to stand close without seeming a pickpocket.

Dark brows, a dissatisfied mouth. She is not by herself by choice. Older than I am; *nu*, so was my wife. Her eyes flicker over the storefronts of Nevsky, searching, alive, not the eyes of a person who lives here. She notices things. She sees beauty. If I do not speak, I'm a coward.

"*Lei Italiana?*" I sound like a madman, my accent absurd. She smiles, her teeth white and impossibly straight.

"*Nyet, Amerikanka.*" American! And she speaks Russian, at least so much as to tell me no in my own language. But she is still smiling, her hand hasn't brushed me away. She is flattered, I think, to be thought European. I must pull some words out of the air, make a contact, no matter how clumsy, before the light takes her away from me.

"This is camera?" I point to the case on her shoulder.

"It's not for sale." Too quickly; she thinks I'm black market.

I shake my head. Don't be wary, don't slam the door. "I am photographer."

"Really?"

No. I'm a liar, a blurter of half-truths to chestnut-haired women about to cross at the streetlight and vanish forever. I would have become a photographer, if I'd had money for film, better scores on my entry exams for the art school, a darkroom in which to develop my visions. Instead I sell shoes. My parents are proud of me, pleased I have work, that my father can walk in a pair of new brogues he could otherwise not afford.

"Yes, I take pictures for magazines."

In my mind's eye. I cannot look at a thing without framing it. Ever since I can remember, my gaze has become its own viewfinder, cropping the edge of a landscape, adjusting the contrast. And now I change lenses, zooming in close as this woman, this sad-eyed American who doesn't know what she could mean to me, brushes a stray wisp of hair that's blown over her parched lips, no lipstick, no hope she'll be kissed.

She knows I am lying. The windbreaker. Talking

too loud, I suppose, like a man who sells cheap shoes. A man who would give all that he has to touch someone who isn't from Russia.

❧

He's cute. Little young for me. What is he asking? *Progulka*? Don't know that one. *Brodit*? Nope, sorry. His eyes are gray-green, with a rim of gold next to the iris. He's gesturing now, one palm flat and two fingers walking across it. *Progulka*! Stroll, yes! Do I want to *progulka* with him along the embankment? Does that sound as dirty to someone who's fluent?

I hope so. I've never felt so unattached. Russians are always in pairs, always touching: soldiers throw their arms around buddies' shoulders, shop girls walk with linked elbows. On the long escalators that lead to the Metro, young couples pair off with the man riding backwards, facing his girl. I like this photographer's face. There's a slight lustful curl to his lip as he waits for my answer; if I nod my head yes, we both know I'm agreeing to more than a stroll.

What the hell, why not have an adventure. It's almost a shame I speak Russian at all; it'd be hotter without a translation. Like that waiter in Portugal. All in the eyes, in the way we moved, every gesture made larger by candlelight. My tongue on the lip of my wineglass. His hand brushing past my bare shoulder, hip pressed to my back as he picked up the platter of mussel shells. Fado music and brine-soaked cobblestones, up a dark stairwell. No small talk. The perfect first date.

But then I was twenty, tanned, drunk on Madeira. I could jump off a cliff just for fun. I still have the urge, but I do look before I leap, even when I'd prefer not to. My wariness isn't a choice, it's an ingrained behavior, worn into my brain like the dip in a stair tread from too many footsteps. I will tell you yes, green eyes, but not all at once.

ಳ

"Do you speak any English?" she asks me.

Oh, *da*. She is willing. "Tiny," I tell her, then add, "But accent is beastly."

She laughs. Such perfect teeth, no gold or silver at all. Her laugh is as loud as a man's, full-chested and throaty, a promise of pleasure. If I used the wrong word, if I'm making myself sound ridiculous, I do not care. As long as she stands here and laughs with me, letting the crowd pass without us. I will show her my Leningrad, untainted by red-letter slogans and government shoe stores. A city designed by a tsar who ached for things foreign, as I do: Venetian canals excavated from swampland, arching footbridges, pilasters and pediments carved for no purpose, which only exist to bring pleasure to those who know how to stroll slowly, who use their whole selves as a camera, recording not only what is, but what could be.

❧

I tell him my name as we walk up the steps to the footbridge, the first piece of foreplay. He savors the foreign syllables, rolling them in his mouth like a fine wine brought by a headwaiter: "Al-li-son." He smiles, a sweet flash of unshaven dimple.

"My name is Nicholas."

"Like the tsar?"

He raises his eyebrows, amused. "He is dead, I am living. My friends call me Kolya."

Okay, so he has a sense of humor, I'll sleep with

him. If I call him Kolya, I'm signing the pact. I wonder how long it will be till he brushes against me as if it's by accident, what part of my body he'll touch.

He stops, leans against the bridge railing. This is my cue to stand just a little too close, make it easy for him. But I don't. I take out my camera. He watches in silent appraisal as I frame the shot. I can't tell if he's looking at me or my Nikon. A gaggle of schoolgirls appears on the sidewalk, their plaits tied in bright chiffon scarves. I wait till they pass a potato-shaped street sweeper and take the picture.

He reaches his hand out. "Now one with you in." I give him my camera. Apparently that's the permission he needs. He guides me towards the bridge rail, his hand lingering on my shoulder, then reaches to brush my hair back with his fingertips.

"Pretty," he says as he fingers my earring. He's looking right into my eyes. I'm not used to this kind of a gaze from a man. I can feel the heat rise in my cheeks.

"*Spasiba,*" I say. "Thank you, Kolya." When he snaps my picture, will he see my lust?

❧

They are firm and high, just as I like them. My wife's breasts were large, looking stern in their harness. Other men noticed them, glancing at me with conspiratorial envy, but in truth they flopped over her chest like a pair of old socks. I wonder what sort of brassiere this American wears. Something silken and edged with lace.

What is she saying? Her Russian is dreadful, a stammering child's. Something about Russian writers, a scene from an opera, so tragic. Yes, lace, I am certain. She looks at me, waiting. It's my turn to speak.

"Russians have a national genius for yearning," I tell her. Allison's eyes look blank. What did she not understand, the words or the sentiment? Suddenly it seems urgent that she knows my thought, that we truly connect. Try to frame it in English.

"Russians, we are liking to sad," I venture. Allison nods with a vigor that proves she did not understand my Russian.

"Yearning." She echoes my word in her charming accent, tracing the rim of her camera lens with her index finger. The knuckle is bruised, the fingernail blunt as a boy's. "So, sad, this means?"

"*Da.*"

April in Leningrad

I want to suck that bruised finger deep into my mouth, run my tongue up her forearm and sink a warm kiss in the pulse of her elbow. I want to feel her breath quicken, to taste her soft skin.

It's a form of emotional chess, to court in a language one doesn't share, chess played by blind men. The strategy may be elegant, but the moves on the board become clumsy, knocking over the bishop while reaching for the knight. In a way it's like every encounter between man and woman, distilled to its essence. The gap between language and thought is so vast we are forced to fill in with a primitive sensing of where we are bound and what stands in our way, like the echolocation of bats.

I offer a *papiros* and she shakes her head, taking one of her own cigarettes from her purse. She proffers the pack as if asking if I'd like to taste one. I would, but I've already clamped my own cardboard filter between my teeth; I don't want to seem greedy. I light a match, holding the flame towards her lips. She leans forward, touching the back of my cupped hand.

☙

He has reddish-brown hair on the back of his hands, nearly up to the knuckles. Does it carpet his chest? Does it sprout from his shoulder blades, march in a dark stripe from navel to groin?

I blow smoke and it twines with his, wafting out over the stone-edged canal.

∽

I show her the stone gryphons carved on my favorite footbridge, the homes of Tchaikovsky and Gogol. She brushes her hair back behind one ear, looking me over. "It seems you are, I don't know how to say it in Russian, nostalgic for past. You are knowing in English, nostalgic?"

Her stress is so different I miss the near-cognate. She riffles through her pocket phrasebook. "Is so hard to talk so, like child," she says, landing her thumb on a word. "Nos-tal-GEE-ya. *Nostalgia.* Almost the same, yes?"

Nostalgic. She is right, in a way, but the past that I long for is not my own. My family would never have dwelled in the Hermitage. Indeed, I could not have been born in the time of the tsars — my father and mother would never have met, never married, she born

April in Leningrad

of White Russians and he from a *shtetl* in Latvia. And if by some miracle I'd been conceived in those times, I would have been even more of an outcast than I am today, falling between two identities like a drunk between stools. A Jewish father is a double curse: you carry the name like a footprint on your back, but the Jews don't acknowledge your bloodline.

If Allison knew I was half Jewish, would she have agreed to this stroll with me? Might she, with her dark eyes, be Jewish herself? I've heard that it's different for Jews in America, but I have no way to find out what I'm longing to know. Do they cringe and feel judged when their surname is spoken aloud? Do they hesitate just at the brink of desire, as a woman's soft fingers slide under their waistband, fearing a circumcised *putz* is the end of the date?

I must ask her home for a glass of tea. We have already taken a full roll of photos. I looked through the lens at her eyes and saw hunger, a loneliness much like my own. She is willing, I know, in the silt of her being, but how do I get there? I don't even have my own tongue; we must quack like ducks, monosyllabic. In this straitened language I've learned that Allison stays only two more days in Leningrad. I cannot afford to be courtly. To woo her by steps is to lose all hope.

But what if she says no? If she looks at this mongrelized Jew in his cheap shoes and windbreaker, not shaved this morning, a red pimple next to his nose like a teenager, amusing enough for a stroll on the Moika but not for the long tram ride home, for the feverish peeling of clothes: a divertissement merely.

How will she put it? "I'd love to, but… ," dipping her head in embarrassment, knowing as I do that she isn't busy, but simply avoiding an unpleasant truth: that I'm not worth the time, or the risk, that I don't measure up. I don't think I can bear one more woman's dismissal. If Allison shrugs me away, I may as well hurl myself over the rail of this bridge. My body will float, cold and bloated, to sea. Here lies Nikolai, worthless.

We are circling back to the place where we met. The sunlight hangs over the street in gold shafts, throwing our shadows in angular stripes against cobblestones: two narrow figures, their hands not quite touching. I must conquer fear. I must stop in my tracks, turn to face her, must push out the words.

"I don't understand," she says, shaking her head.

"*Chashka chayu*," I sputter. The English phrase jumps into memory, unbidden. "A spot of tea." Allison laughs. Have I said something stupid?

"*Da*," she says. Yes. She will come. My head rings with the very unlikeliness of it, this lovely American girl setting foot in my flat, like a tropical bird in a feeder of sparrows.

❧

The escalator descends to the Metro. As we glide under the sign that says cameras are strictly forbidden, Kolya moves down to the next step, then turns back to face me. It's happened. I am part of a Russian pairing, no longer estranged from the coupled-off world.

Should I have called Susan, left word with the hostile hotel clerk? I'm putting my trust in somebody I've known for an hour; I am leaving not even a breadcrumb by which anybody could trace my steps. Bringing him to our hotel room was out of the question. Susan is working, might even be holding a phone interview for her magazine piece. Our arrangement is simple: I leave in the morning and come back at night. She is here on assignment, and I'm the invisible roommate. In less than a week I've seen every museum in Leningrad, sidestepped countless black marketeers, run nine rolls of film through the Nikon. In the evening she's taken me drinking with journalists, who lose interest as soon as they learn that I don't have a byline. Kolya has not even asked what I do for a living. For that fact alone, I could kiss him.

The station is huge as a ballroom, with real chandeliers, marble columns and no advertisements. For somebody used to the cracked tiles and stench of the BMT, it is eerily elegant, as if we have entered an underground palace. Kolya takes hold of my arm as our train burrows inwards. I step through its doors and fall off my own map.

❧

She sits on the bench and I stand guard in front of her. Everyone on this train looks inert, beaten down by the pettiness of his own life. A woman with warts on her forehead and one gold front tooth clutches a string bag of cucumber plants. Two slab-faced young soldiers stare off into space. A snoring drunk lolls so far to one side that his bag of groceries falls over, spilling turnips all over the floor of the train. Oy, what my country must look like to Allison. What she will think of my room, wedged behind my parents' refrigerator in their cluttered flat. Did I make the bed? Doubtful. Well, nothing to do about that. I must simply rejoice that she said yes at all.

♋

Okay, where the hell are we? We got out of the Metro and onto a tram. Then the bus. We've been on it at least half an hour and I have no clue how to find my way back to the Metro station, much less the hotel. Where is Kolya's apartment, Siberia? This is a total mistake. He's probably a psychopath. He could stab me and steal my camera, the money I changed at the Intourist desk, my American passport.

He's talking to me. Those are lips made for kissing, so shiny inside, a moist promise. His front teeth are stained from those, what are they called, *papirosi*? The half-cardboard cigarettes, Camels on speed. Should I tell him I don't understand, or just smile and nod? He puts his hands onto my shoulders, urging me forward. The bus doors hiss open and shudder as we step outside.

This is it? Each building a full block of unadorned windows and cracked gray cement. It's the projects, the rind of the city. There's some kind of salt marsh behind us, a bare dirt path winding through weeds. A skeletal crane in the gash of a new excavation. This must be where the hacked bodies of tourists wind up. I wonder when Susan would notice. She knows me too well to worry if I don't make it back to the hotel tonight. Ever since college, she's been with some guy in a long-running couple and I've been out picking up strays.

It is way, way too late to do anything else but go through with this. Back at the tram transfer, I had a choice. Now I'm in Kolya's hairy-backed hands.

&

Not even in my ugly language is there a word for the consummate ugliness of these apartments, these Socialist warts on the face of old Petersburg. If Gorbachev wants to impress us with his Perestroika, he should start by rebuilding our homes. When I met Allison, she had just come from the Hermitage, her eyes still agleam from its vaulted gilt ceilings and vast chandeliers, pouring crystal like fountains. Now she is coming to my cement mouse hole. I hope that my father will not act pathetic. I hope I have biscuits for tea. I hope I have tea.

I ought to have asked her to stop into one of the dollar stores — we could have feasted on caviar, chocolates — but one shudders to ask such a favor. She is so beautiful, Allison, with her English name from the song that I heard on a bootleg, a knock-kneed man wearing large glasses. Her eyes flicker over the salt marsh, the distant flat gray of the Gulf of Finland. She reaches for something. Perhaps one of her very peculiar American cigarettes, smelling of mint, carried from New York City.

Oy God, it's her camera she's taking out. Why would she photograph this? There is nothing. No eye could be pleased with this landscape. And people are strolling here, two by two, out for a breath of fresh air before they climb five flights of stairs, cursing the lift that's been broken all summer, to boil cabbage soup for their children. They are already looking at us; they will certainly notice her foreign-made camera. But Allison has none of our wariness. Look how she swings the camera right up to her eye, no reflex to check for the neighbor whom everyone says is a secret policeman, no worries about what's permitted. Such freedom you can't buy with rubles. It is this that I want to lick off her skin, that I want to make love to inside my gray room.

So there's graffiti in Russia; who knew? The elevator isn't working — the sign on its door, *Remont*, is one I can read on sight after a week in this city where everything modern appears to be broken. The back stairs smell of urine and cabbage. The scrawls on the paint look like tags on the brick walls of Avenue B. I wonder if Soviet teens form gangs, if they hawk drugs, run numbers, what music they play. I wonder how I can be thinking about this as I tail a virtual stranger up four flights of poorly lit stairs.

❦

If one believed in a God, one could pray that one's parents would not be at home, that one's mother would not shuffle forth in house slippers exclaiming, "My darling!" then frown upon realizing that one has not only forgotten the two loaves of bread and chopped meat, but has brought home instead an American girl in a black leather jacket. One could pray that one's out-of-work father would be lying in bed like a goggle-eyed fish and would not hear one's key as it turned in the lock.

One could pray, but one's God would not prove to be listening. For here comes my mother, still dressed in her lab coat, involuntarily pausing mid-motion as she sees a stranger cross over the threshold, the knee-jerk suspicion that someone's in trouble.

"Mama," I say, hoping it doesn't sound childish to my surprised guest, "This is Allison. She's from America."

Mama's eyebrows twist upwards, twin question marks. "Does she speak Russian?"

"A little," says Allison in her flat accent, as my father's tobacco-strained bleat rises out of his bedroom, "America?" I hear lurching bedsprings, his feet thumping onto the floor. I grab Allison's hand and propel her towards my room before he can make his way into the kitchen, a vision in phlegm and long underwear. She smiles crookedly at my mother, intoning "good night." It's "good evening" she means, but her usage, I hope, has a deeper truth: Russians say good night only when we head for bed.

❧

He lives with his *parents*? I thought he said

he was divorced. What else have I misunderstood, plugging up language gaps with wishful thinking? His room is a teenager's pigsty: a landslide of twisted sheets, magazines, socks, album covers, old coffee cups. Where is his camera, his darkroom equipment? There's one goddamned photo, a stock shot of Venetian gondolas, hung on the wall. Beside it, a map of the London Underground, a street sign in German, a soccer ball with a Brazilian flag: a shrine to the world outside Russia. Is that what I am, then, a trophy head for a collector of foreigners? This is not what I meant by adventure.

Nothing ever works out. Even my Portuguese waiter had filthy dishes stacked up on the counter, a toilet that reeked. He was sweaty and rough during sex, and dismissive as soon as the sun rose; I didn't fit into his day. It's the wave of desire I remember, not the return to sand. Waves crest and break; that's what makes them waves. Maybe that's all we can have.

Turn to me, Kolya. If you pull me close, if you kiss me so hard that my temperature rises, I can forget about balled socks and magazines under the bed, your mother's snap judgment the instant she saw me, the rattling fridge I can hear through the wall.

April in Leningrad

He puts on a record. The grooves hiss and crackle. "I hope you will like this," he says. "It is music by gypsies." A tingle of mandolin, guttural scrape of a violin bow, and a woman's voice levitates, keening with heartbreak. I take a step towards him. He dives for the kiss like a man who's been starving, his tongue warm and ready, tasting sweet underneath the stale odor of cheap cigarettes. He peels off my jacket, then pauses to fold it with what seems like reverence, placing it over the back of a chair. So tender, this gesture. All right, then. Why not?

❧

When I turn back, her sweater is off. My heart tries to break through my rib cage. Not lacy at all, but gray cotton with wide white elastic like men's undershorts, an incomprehensible garment, as drab as a pigeon. I pull her close, feeling her breasts swell against my chest. Her fingers slide under my shirt, moving upwards like fever. I bury my lips in her neck, breathe the citrus perfume of her hair. There's a knock at the door. It's my father. "Kolyushka?" His voice is obsequious, cringing.

"Later!" I snap, but it's too late: he's opened the door.

The old man turns crimson and slams the door quickly. Kolya curses. I wish I could sink through the rug. I've been in his room, what, five minutes? And I'm standing here with my shirt off. I reach for my sweater, shaking my head. "It's not a good time."

Kolya's voice rises, pleading. "No, please, just forget him. I'll lock the door, see? We're alone."

"No we aren't. They're standing right there. I just don't feel — "

"Allison, please. This is how we live. This is Russian privacy."

He may well be telling the truth — the dissident Susan is writing about lives in a communal apartment with three other families; he brings home his mistress right under their nose. But it isn't *my* truth. I feel soiled and embarrassed, too old to be caught in the act by somebody's parents. I reach for my purse.

"Don't leave." There is such constrained rage in his voice, such a desperate pleading. I hesitate, holding my camera. If I were at home, I'd already be pounding a hasty retreat down the tenement stairwell, en route to the subway. But I'm not at home. I'm thousands of miles from the BMT local, with someone whose everyday life, like an old-country saga of hardship, includes making love only inches away from the relatives. How did lovers manage in one-room huts, straw-ticking mattresses shared by whole households? Did they learn to shut out everything but their mates, or find an illicit thrill in coupling amid the peripheral snores and criss-crossing limbs of their forebears?

I can't bear to let Kolya down. No, let's be honest: I can't bear to let myself down. How long has it been since a man picked me up on the street, looking at me with unambivalent ardor? I got onto the tram, after all; I can swallow what little is left of my pride. If I leave here now, I leave with nothing. A long ride back home steeped in shame and self-pity, one more log for the bonfire of missed opportunities that my life has become. I can strain out the details like stray leaves of tea when I retell the events of this day to myself: an afternoon romance in Leningrad, a green-eyed young lover.

Why settle for bitterness? Why give this up? There is someone before me who wants to make love, who desires me this moment. When I lift my face up towards Kolya's, he practically weeps. I can feel every vein in his neck as he clutches me, wrapping my body around his so tightly my feet leave the floor.

She's here, she's not leaving, she's bending to take off her pants. It's a miracle. This is why people invented a God. I reach for my own straining zipper, prepared to expose my pink yarmulke. What do Americans do about birth control? I've read of a new disease there that spreads through sex; what if she's carrying it? I might still have a condom or two in my drawer, since Ludmila, the cow, doubled up with her diaphragm during her most fertile days. Will I offend Allison if I take it out?

"Oh good," she says, reaching to take the foil packet. "I don't have one with me." She peels back the foil and removes the thing expertly. Is she going to put it on for me? Ludmila would never have dreamed such a thing. The thought of Allison's hands on my penis expands its erection. I hold my breath as she sets the brittle balloon on its tip and begins to unroll, without comment on my lack of foreskin. Is every American girl so compliant, so matter-of-fact? I am swollen with joy as her unashamed fingers move downwards, a tickling dance.

"Oh, shit," she blurts. I open my eyes and look down. The Soviet condom has split in half.

Damn this country, to sabotage even the most private ecstasy with its incompetence! That's my last condom. I curse in a helpless explosion. "It's okay," Allison soothes me, "This is now not my bad part of month." She moves my hand into the hollow between her thighs. I will risk anything, death or disease. I am yours, my miraculous Allison, yours, all yours.

❧

Twilight hovers, the room a gray mist. How long has the record been doing that, swish of the needle on empty grooves, bumping the label again and again? Kolya gets up, his spinal bumps knobby, his muscular buttocks so pale. There are patches of hair in the small of his back, like a threadbare stuffed animal. He lifts up the tone arm and comes back to bed. He sits next to my pillow, cupping his palm over one of my breasts. "You'd like tea now?" He's smiling.

"No tea," I say, dreading the opening door, the emergence back into his parents' cramped kitchen.

Let me hold onto this sweetness, this fleeting reprieve from the day's disappointments, the rest of my life. Let Kolya's fingers bring warmth to my skin, let him hold me again so that we can pretend, just a few moments longer, that sharing a touch in the dark is enough.

❦

Never have I been so happy to lie with a woman, to feel my sweat glazing her skin like the dew on a garden. I am full, I am new, I am hope itself. We will have two days together. Two days and two nights. What my life would be like if she'd only come back, if she'd marry me. If.

The Memorable Memo

by

Catherine Onyemelukwe

One afternoon in November 1963, well into my second year as a Peace Corps Volunteer in Nigeria, I was surprised to find a memo from the chief electrical engineer of the Electricity Corporation of Nigeria under my door.

"ECN is conducting a survey of electricity usage in Ikoyi," it said. Ikoyi was the residential area of Lagos where I lived. "You were not present when our inspectors came to your flat. You are asked to report to the Chief Electrical Engineer's office at ECN headquarters."

My government-furnished apartment came with overhead lights, a fridge, a water heater, and a ceiling fan in the living room. I had bought an iron and a radio that was frequently on when I was home, but I wasn't home much. The stove was gas.

I was nervous. They might cut off my electricity if I didn't comply. The next day, after I finished teaching, I drove to ECN.

I knew the building along Lagos Marina, a main thoroughfare into downtown. Women in blue, green and red cotton wrappers and head ties, some with babies tied on their backs, hurried past, in sharp contrast to men in suits entering the building.

I marched in. "The chief engineer is on the seventh floor," a receptionist told me. "I will tell his secretary you are coming."

I found the office and the secretary, a middle-aged Nigerian woman in a stiff blue satin head tie. "I received this notice." I held it out to her as if it held poison.

"Please wait here," she said. She returned quickly. "The chief engineer will see you now." She showed me into his office. I saw a serious looking Nigerian man who was dwarfed by the immensity of the space. He looked young, maybe around thirty. He sat in a black leather chair behind a polished wood desk. He had a roundish face that reminded me of a koala bear, and wore a dark wool business suit, white shirt, tie, and pocket handkerchief.

"Please sit down." He gestured to the chair in front of his desk. "Thank you for coming in."

"Why am I getting this notice?" I said. "I'm a Peace Corps Volunteer. I have an iron I hardly use, and a radio I sometimes play, and a fridge, and lights — that's all my electricity usage!"

"We have no wish to make you angry," he said. "My staff is conducting this survey to check on unauthorized connections and the problem of overload. I'm sorry if you are upset."

I stayed only long enough to be assured that my electricity would not be cut off.

On the following Saturday afternoon I was preparing the next week's lesson plans before getting dressed to go out when there was a knock at my door.

I wasn't surprised to see Grace Ewulu, whom I'd met several times before. I was pleased that I fit in so well that Nigerians felt they could just come by without notice, as was customary.

Beside her there was a casually dressed man. "This is Clement Onyemelukwe, a friend of ours," she said. "I've been meaning to call so I took advantage of his visit to ask him to bring me here."

"You don't remember me, do you?" he said. I shook my head. "You were in my office a few days ago, and you were not happy. In fact, you were actually a little rude!"

"Oh, you're the chief electrical engineer?" I was embarrassed. "Yes, I was annoyed. Was I really rude?"

With his informal dress and without the official setting, he looked different. I recalled the koala bear image that had struck me. I also noticed his smile. I thought he could be someone I'd like to know better.

"I'll take that as an apology," he said. I remembered that Grace didn't drive, so her explanation of their visit made sense.

"What would you like to drink?" I said after they were seated. "I have fresh palm wine."

"Where did you get that?" Clem said.

"Didn't you see the palm tree right outside my window? The tapper was here this morning. I usually buy when I see him." I brought glasses and the palm wine from the kitchen and poured them each a glassful.

We talked about her son who was a student at my school, the country's need for electricity, and Clem's life in Britain before he returned to Nigeria two years before.

"Would you like to come to my house next Saturday evening? I'm having a party," Clem said, looking from me to her.

I liked the idea of spending time with him and readily agreed. I would pick up Grace, who knew where his house was. I heard nothing more about the inspection of my electricity. I didn't learn why until years later.

I dressed carefully for the party, in a black linen embroidered dress and low heels. Clem mixed with other guests but spent the majority of his time at my side. He was easy to be with, and I was pleased when he asked me to go out with him. We dated several times in the next five weeks, usually going to the cinema and sometimes to dinner as well. We visited a couple of his friends who were married to English women. I liked his friends, and found myself liking him more and more.

Before Christmas, my school held an event for which I'd agreed to be in charge of the food. Clem suggested he drop me off and pick me up afterwards.

"It was a disaster," I said as I got into his Ford Consul. "The food was delivered late, and there weren't enough large plates."

"Did everyone get something to eat?"

"Yes, but it took too long."

"Don't worry. You agreed to a difficult task, and everyone ate. That's all they'll remember." He provided the comfort and reassurance I needed.

Later that evening, I said, "I'm going to Enugu right after Christmas to work at a day camp with other Peace Corps Volunteers."

"My cousin Isaiah lives in Enugu. I'll call him and

Catherine Onyemelukwe

tell him you are coming," Clem said. "He studied in the US. He would be happy to meet an American. He can show you around."

"That would be great. I want to see some of the region," I said.

On December 26, Clem drove me to the taxi park.

"Ready to go! Board now! Best price!" shouted the touts rounding up passengers for the Peugeot 404s and larger buses. Families with children, women carrying chickens, and men holding bundles of cloth were all bargaining for the lowest price and the best seats. Clem helped me negotiate with one of the touts for a spot in the front seat of a Peugeot.

Squeezed next to the driver and another passenger, with three passengers on each of the other three seats, I sped out of Lagos. The sour smell of so many sweaty bodies in the heat was intense. December Harmattan haze hung in the air and added dust to the smell.

I reached Enugu and checked into the Peace Corps rest house, where Isaiah came for me on Saturday. He resembled Clem with the round face, but was taller and more outgoing. He wore a dashiki, a loose V-neck cotton shirt with a diamond pattern in red, white, green, blue, and yellow, called "the keyhole."

"Have you been to Onitsha?" he asked, as I got into his VW bug.

"I've been through it, but never really seen it," I said. "I'd like to."

We drove up the five-mile Milliken Hill, on a narrow, curving two-lane road. It was in poor condition, and he was a nervous driver. His frequent gear-shifting and haphazard control of the gas pedal imitated his slight stutter and frequent laughter, and left me feeling car sick.

I was not reassured by having no guard rails at the side of the road. I could look down hundreds of feet through the trees. I saw one lorry that clearly had missed the curve. I wondered what it would feel like to go over the edge. And I wondered how I would survive the drive back.

At the crest of Milliken Hill the terrain leveled out.

"I'm taking you to Clem's family," he said. "They want to meet you. And it will give you the opportunity to see real people of the region, in their own home," he said. I bought that explanation. I was certainly naïve. His story was as true as the survey of electricity use, I learned years later.

I looked forward to meeting an Ibo family.

Knowing their son was a bonus that would make the meeting more fun.

We drove through Awka, with its famous carved wooden doors outside vendors' shops. In another half hour we entered Onitsha, which had none of the government buildings I had seen in Enugu or Lagos. It did have an impressive Anglican cathedral that would have looked at home in any large British city. It dominated a major intersection with its gray mass, stained glass windows, and tall steeple. Across the street was the slightly rundown Dennis Memorial Grammar School. Isaiah said, "Clement and our cousin Jonathan were together at DMGS; I was there later."

"Did they board at the school?"

"No," he said. "Clem's parents couldn't afford that. They walked from their house, where we're going." Clem had told me how he had excelled in his secondary school. I knew he would be pleased that I had seen it.

We turned down a poorly maintained street with a Roman Catholic church and stucco houses. They all looked in need of paint. Many had market stalls in the front yard and businesses on the ground floor — vehicle repair shops, typing centers, tire sales, and sewing or tailoring establishments. The sounds of

The Memorable Memo

talking, laughter, and car horns mingled with shouts of small children playing. Older children carried goods for sale on their heads. After two more turns on streets getting progressively worse, we were at the house Clem had described. I was intrigued by the street name — St. John's Cross.

The yard was bare of grass, but a flame tree and a few straggly bushes grew in the reddish-brown soil. The house was a single-story building of cement blocks covered with stucco, set back about ten feet. The dimpled exterior had remnants of yellow paint from long ago. The windows had no glass. Instead, there were wooden shutters, open during the day.

As we got out of the car, children called out "*Onye ocha*! White person!" We crossed the narrow board laid across the three-foot-wide gutter, mounted the two steps, and entered the living room, dim after the bright sun outside. There were dusty curtains at the windows, a smooth mud floor, and a low ceiling. Clem's mother met us. She had the same round face and shy smile as Clem. She wore a red and blue wrapper and matching *buba* or blouse, in a cotton Dutch print. Isaiah hugged her warmly, calling her "Mama."

Clem's father looked distinguished in a long beige

embroidered top, cotton trousers and leather sandals like those sold by the Hausa traders I saw in Lagos. Several young people peered at us from the back room. Isaiah addressed Clem's father as "Papa," and they shook hands. I was a little puzzled — these were not his parents, were they? Then I remembered that Isaiah had told me his parents had died long ago, so maybe he regarded them as stand-ins.

He introduced me and I shook hands. I had no idea what he said to them in Ibo. Was he saying I was Clement's acquaintance, friend, or girlfriend?

"*Nno*, welcome," they said to me. "*Kedu*? How are you?" they asked, and I replied politely to their mixture of Ibo and stilted English.

"Sit down," Papa said. There was a dilapidated two-seater sofa, and three wooden chairs. Isaiah took a seat on the sofa while I chose a chair.

Papa spoke to one of the children who came in a moment later with pinkish-gray kola nuts, green "garden eggs," and a large dab of what looked like peanut butter, on a tray. "Guests are always given kola as a welcome," Isaiah said as he took the tray from Papa to show to each of us before handing it back. Papa took one of the kola nuts, and holding it aloft, spoke a few sentences in Ibo. "He's praising God, thanking him for the kola and for our safe journey," Isaiah said. I was glad; with Isaiah's driving, we should have been very grateful.

Then he broke the kola nuts into several pieces, and asked Isaiah to pass the tray around. "Take one but watch out for the garnish!" Isaiah said. I took a piece and used it to grasp a small dollop of the peanut butter. I bit into it, and my mouth was on fire. This was no ordinary peanut butter. The bitter nut couldn't overcome the burning sensation. My eyes started to water as I swallowed.

"*Ndo*, sorry," Mama said. "Is pepper too much?" I could only gasp and nod my head. After the kola was passed and everyone had taken their own, Mama called another child who went out the door and returned a few moments later with soft drinks. I was grateful for the cold Coke to cool my red-hot throat.

"How be Clement?" Mama said.

"He's fine," I said. "He sends his greetings," a small lie since I hadn't known I would meet them.

"How be work?" Clem's mother said. I explained my teaching, with Isaiah translating. Clem's parents watched me intently. I learned later that they were sizing me up against the Ibo women they had been sending to him since his return from the UK two years earlier, hoping he would choose one to marry. Here was a strange young white woman he had sent to them.

"How is family?" I said to Mama. Her response was to call Clem's siblings and introduce them. They wore Western dress, the girls in colorful blouses and skirts, and the boy in a sports shirt and khaki pants. Grace was in nursing school, she said, and Geoffrey was in secondary school. The youngest, Nebechi, had just finished primary school and was awaiting her Common Entrance Examination results.

"Where do you go to nursing school?" I asked Grace.

"Benin," was her short answer. I followed with Geoffrey.

"Government College Umuahia." I had already heard about the fierce rivalry between Clem's *alma mater*, Dennis Memorial Grammar School, and Umuahia.

"You didn't choose DMGS like Clem?"

"Umuahia is better," he said with a smile.

The children disappeared again, though I saw them watching from the back. Isaiah kept the conversation going, occasionally directing a question to me about Lagos. I was proud just to be there, able to feel comfortable with an Ibo family, sharing the kola ceremony and meeting the children.

When we had stayed for an hour and a half, Isaiah said, "We should leave, so we have time to visit Nanka before night."

He turned to me. "In Nanka you will see a real Ibo village, mud huts and all."

As we drove out of Onitsha, Isaiah described the village, the family members I would meet, and their family's role in village life. I learned that the town of Nanka has seven villages; their own was called Enugu Nanka. "We Onyemelukwes are well known in Nanka," he said. "The whole town is proud of Clement as the first Nigerian chief engineer in ECN. We are thought of as leaders, with me having a BA in economics, Clement with his BSc, engineering, and Jonathan as a priest."

He said Ejike was the patriarch of the family, the oldest of five sons. "Ejike and his wife Obele will be there. Another brother and his wife live very near so you will meet them, too."

He pointed out Agulu, the town Clem's mother was from. The buildings and trees that lined the road were covered by reddish-brown dust. Soon he announced that we had entered Nanka. A large Anglican church anchored the corner where we turned. It was an anomaly amongst the ramshackle wooden structures and market stalls that bordered the other side of the road.

"This is the town shrine," Isaiah said as we rounded a bend, indicating an enclosure on our left. Bamboo poles held the thatch roof in place. I could see an altar at the center. "The church was built opposite to diminish the importance of the traditional religion," he said as he pointed back at the church. "The church has won, but some of the elders still visit the shrine to communicate with ancestors."

We followed the dirt road downhill for three miles. We passed thatch-roofed huts, interspersed with occasional tin-covered houses of the same reddish-brown mud, banana and palm trees, and fields of what I later learned were yams, corn, and cassava.

"The entrance is around the back," Isaiah said, as he parked by a six-foot-high mud wall. I followed him for about 100 feet along a path bordered by the wall on our left and cultivated fields on the right. Five or six children appeared, calling the now familiar, "*Onye ocha*, white person!" A couple wore tattered shorts, others were naked. We turned left for another thirty feet, following the wall, and then reached the entrance.

Isaiah pushed open the carved wooden door. We had to step over a raised earthen step and crouch at the same time to pass under a wooden frame over the door. The children hung around outside the entrance, watching.

I noticed a faint acrid odor. Then I saw the goats in their shed on the left. Just beyond them was an eight-foot-high open structure of bamboo poles, holding yams. On the right there was a deep hole about six feet in diameter, protected by a low mud wall.

At the center of the compound was a square, thatch-roofed mud hut. "This is the *obi*, the spiritual center for the family," Isaiah said as a man emerged. He was about five-foot-ten, slender and muscular. As we approached him, I couldn't avoid staring at his facial markings: several horizontal striations on his forehead and others that started near his eyes and extended down to his chin. He wore khaki shorts, a loose shirt, and striped wool cap like a child's snow hat.

After exchanging greetings, Isaiah introduced me. I don't know what he said, but many years later, I was told he said, "This is the white woman that Clement wants to marry." I said, "*Kedu? Kedu maka ndi be gi?* How are you, and how is your family?" as Isaiah had taught me on the way. Ejike exploded with laughter and shouts.

I spotted a woman hovering at the doorway of another smaller hut, to the left of the *obi*. This was a rectangle with a lower thatch roof. Isaiah had told me that Ejike's wife was Obele. I guessed this was her house. She wore a dark wrapper and blouse.

Ejike invited us to enter his hut, which had the same rust-colored mud walls about four feet high. We sat on the mud bench built into the inside wall while he took the carved wooden chair. It was cooler inside, with a thatch roof at least sixteen feet high at the center, sloping down to hang over the walls. Rather scary objects hung from the wooden beams. As my eyes adjusted to the darkness, I could identify cow horns and what looked like skulls of small mammals.

He shouted and a teenage boy appeared, listened, and disappeared again. He returned a moment later with kola nuts. I was relieved that there was no peanut butter-like substance.

Out of the corner of my eye I saw that a group of children had gathered inside the compound, clearly afraid to approach closely. Again, Isaiah was given the tray of kola nuts to show to me. He returned it to Ejike who held one up as he spoke in his deep voice. Isaiah translated. "Bless this kola, and bless our ancestors who gave us life." He then waved the kola toward us. "Thank you for the safe journey of these visitors. Bless our son Clement and the others who are far away today." He broke the kola nuts, gave the tray to Isaiah to pass, and then waited for him to explain our visit. I heard the name "Clement," a few times, but that was all I understood.

Then he reached down and lifted a calabash of palm wine. He shouted something.

"He's calling his wife, Obele," Isaiah said. She came in with a couple of glasses, while Ejike took a cow's horn from a battered black briefcase. I wondered whether the palm wine he was pouring was safe to drink. When I bought it in Lagos it came straight from the tapper to my fridge. But Isaiah and Ejike were drinking it, so why shouldn't I? I accepted a glass, and sipped at it. The men downed theirs in one draught.

A younger man resembling Ejike without the facial markings and with a slightly heavier build arrived, and I was introduced to Obi, Clem's youngest uncle. Isaiah pointed out his wife Mercy, who had followed him but didn't enter the *obi*. This was the real thing: a village, an extended family, the naked little children, the goats, the mud huts.

The wall that encircled the compound was broken only by a third building, halfway in Ejike's compound and halfway in the next, and a gate that led into the adjoining compound. Isaiah took me through. "Clem sends money to his father, as a dutiful son should. He doesn't know that his father is using the money to build this." I saw a partially completed, modern two-story house with a veranda. "You can tell him," Isaiah said.

We made our farewells, and as we walked back to the car, still trailed by children, I offered to drive back. Thank goodness he accepted, so the ride itself was more pleasant. I thanked him for giving me this fascinating look at Onitsha and Nanka, and background about the people we met. The last thing on my mind was that this village, this family and all the people I had met would become part of my life.

When I got back to Lagos, I told Clem, "Isaiah was great. I loved meeting your parents and Grace, Geoffrey and Nebechi. The children were shy and wouldn't talk to me."

"I hardly know them," Clem said. "They were so little when I left for England. I think Nebechi was only one or two."

"Did you know your father is building a house in Nanka?"

"No. Did you see it?"

I assured him I had.

That very week, my Fiat broke down on the way home from my village school. I abandoned it on Carter Bridge and took a taxi to Clem's house. He arranged for it to be picked up and repaired, and then shortened his working day to drive me the fifteen miles each way for several days, until it was fixed. This was an unexpected kindness. Our conversations became livelier and more intimate. I began spending nights with him.

Two months later, we were driving along the Lagos Marina on our way to dinner at the Bristol Hotel, when I said, "Why did you ask Isaiah to take me to Onitsha and to the village?"

"If you must know, it's because I want to marry you!"

I sat bolt upright. "You could have asked me first," I said.

"Forget it," he said angrily. "We don't have to talk about marriage again."

"I didn't say we shouldn't talk about it. I just said you should ask me, not assume."

We arrived at Bristol Hotel, parked, and made our way to the dining room in silence. Clem snapped at the waiter for being slow to bring menus. I was relieved he was directing his anger at someone besides me, but I felt sorry for the unsuspecting waiter who was in the line of fire. I had begun ordering for him at restaurants, but this night he chose and ordered for himself. No discussion of sharing an appetizer, no pondering which entrées to choose.

Our conversation was limited to my asking, "How is your food?" I got a gruff, "Fine." I barely touched my lamb chops. We didn't order dessert. He paid the bill and we departed as quietly as we'd come.

I wasn't sure I wanted to go home with him. He didn't ask. Still not talking, he pulled into his driveway and got out, walked into the house, barely waiting for me, and went straight upstairs. As we were getting into bed, his anger was palpable. "I'm sorry I took you unawares," I said. "I didn't mean to upset you."

"Well, you did." He rehashed the whole conversation, pointing out my error in asking him to explain why Isaiah had taken me to see his parents. What error? I had asked an innocent question. If he had felt attacked, wasn't that his problem?

As I listened, I realized that it was my problem too. I'd known him barely five months. Yet I loved him and hated to see him unhappy.

Gradually he calmed down. "I didn't mean to say what I did," he said. "It just popped out of my mouth. It won't happen again."

"That's not what I want. I just said you should ask me, not take me for granted."

"Well, I'll have to think about it," he said, taking my hand.

"When you're sure, let me know," I said, turning to kiss him.

We touched the subject gingerly again a week later, and I could tell he wanted to ask me. But he didn't seem ready to make a proper proposal, so I waited. I needed time to think. I felt sure I'd say yes when he finally asked, but was I being too naïve?

The obvious question — whether an interracial, intercultural marriage could work — I had seen answered by Clem's friends. Of course it could. I would learn Ibo like Jean. I would get to know his family and he would get to know mine. We would visit his village often but not live there. I would continue teaching.

I talked to Lucy, a friend from Cameroon, who said, "If you're going to marry a Nigerian, an Ibo is the best choice. They are more likely to be faithful." I knew the reputation of Nigerian men as philanderers, so her comment gave me somewhat back-handed relief.

At a library conference two weeks after Clem's blow-up at his inadvertent comment, I ran into my friend John Harris from Ibadan, who knew the country and its people well. He asked the obvious question, the same one I had at the top of my mind. "Do you love him enough to make this commitment?" And I gave him the answer that was already clear in my mind. I did.

In late March, we were getting into bed when he said, "There's something I want to discuss with you." Not a very romantic opening, but I could tell what was coming "You have shown me that you respect my culture and my people," he said. "You are adaptable and appear to be content living here. Is that true?"

"Yes, that's all true. I do respect your culture and your people." For good measure and in anticipation of his question, I said, "I am very happy living here."

Then he said it. "I love you, and I want you to be my wife."

"Are you sure?" I teased. "I'm not just forcing you to say this?"

"Don't joke," he said. "I'm very sure. I mean every word."

"Then I accept," I said, as I snuggled close to him.

"I love you, too."

I loved Clem and he loved me. Nigeria felt like home, a place I could continue to make my own. I was excited as I began making plans. My Peace Corps service would finish in June. Peace Corps would send me home to the US. Then I would come back on my own. We would marry in December.

Twelve years later, Clem had his own engineering business. I was reading one evening and he was writing a memo to send about an increase in the price of steel. It was addressed as if it were going to many people. I said, "Don't you only have one client this memo is for? Why don't you just write to them?"

"Yes, it's only one," he said. "But it looks more impressive and the price increase is more palatable to have it come as an official memo."

That suddenly reminded me of the memo that led me to his office so many years earlier. "How many people got the memo about the electricity survey twelve years ago?"

"What do you mean?" he said, refusing to look me in the eye.

"You know perfectly well what I mean."

"You were the only one," he said. "I saw you at the

Mobil gas station on Awolowo Road. I followed you home."

"You made up the memo and delivered it yourself?"

"You looked so attractive," he said. "I was only looking for a little fun."

"But I was rude and left your office without any plan to see you again. So how did you manage to visit me?"

"What could I do?" he said. "I asked around at the flats where you lived." He shifted on his side of the bed. "When they told me you taught at the Emergency Science School, I remembered my friend Mrs. Ewulu. I thought she might know you.

"So she was part of the scam?"

"See where it got you!" he said, as he leaned over to kiss me.

The Upside Down Trees

by

Doreen E. Massey

The cruise ship, *Alaskan Hero*, sidled into Juneau at dawn on September 1, four days after leaving Vancouver. A low mist, penetrated by splinters of harbor lights, veiled the dock, where tourist kiosks were opening and buses lined up for the day's excursions.

Lilian leaned against the rail of her balcony on the veranda deck and shivered. Seagulls screeched and jabbed their heads, rolling as they walked, pecking and squabbling over bits of food. The Alaskan flag flopped round a pole, but she could make out the eight gold stars on the dark blue background — the emblem and hope of Alaska, designed by a young Aleut boy in 1927.

Lilian had chosen to see the Glacier Gardens Rainforest and the Mendenhall Glacier. She showered in the tiny cubicle in her cabin and dressed to go up to the self-service restaurant for a quick breakfast. Two young men were eating scrambled eggs and bacon. They smiled and said they were going rock climbing.

She dressed warmly and coiled round her neck the possum wool scarf Geoff had bought for her two years ago in New Zealand. She held it to her face and breathed in its warmth through the soft, prickly threads.

She still expected Geoff to be there when she turned round, still expected him to walk through a door, to want to share grand plans and small incidents, talk about the children, school, the garden or sit doing a crossword over a weekend coffee. But Geoff left her for another woman last year. They were married for almost forty years.

The bus headed for the Glacier Gardens Rainforest outside Juneau. The sun was rising, mist evaporating from trees and hills. The pine forests smelled glutinous and heavy. In a month's time, all tours would end and, shortly after, a hundred inches of snow would cover this landscape, with a hundred feet on Mount McKinley in the north.

The guide book said that, ten years ago, there had been a landslide in the Glacier Gardens due to heavy rain. The tall, old trees, mainly spruce and pine, were uprooted and slid down the hills. The owner of the land lopped off the branches, and embedded the trees upside down in the earth, with waterproof material

The Upside Down Trees

wrapped round the trunks up to fifteen feet. The thick, tapering roots now formed the tops of the trees, and spread out like tentacles. He placed sphagnum moss and earth amongst them and planted flowers and foliage: petunias, fuchsias and ground ivy, which the Americans call Creeping Charlie. The mature plants now tumbled down the trunks, tousled and exuberant.

Lilian ran her hand up a scaly tree trunk and dug her fingers into the fissures. A voice behind her said, "Well, I've heard of upside down cake, but not trees."

She was surprised to hear someone say, in an English accent, what she was thinking.

"I know," she said. "I've never seen anything like it. I may try it out in my own garden, except that it's too small."

They introduced themselves. Lilian and Philip. He was from Gloucestershire. They were both traveling alone and on the same ship. He was leaving the tour at Seward and she going inland to Denali National Park.

He seemed slightly older than her, with a wide, tanned face, lined around the mouth and eyes. His white hair curled over his ears. He had broad hands with slender fingers; he wore a signet ring, but no wedding ring.

He suggested that they find coffee in the tourist center, part of a vast greenhouse. They entered the musty, succulent smell. Bougainvillea was trained up trellises and poked out crimson and purple flowers. Palms stretched to the glass ceiling, ferns and bright orchids covered the raised beds. Creeping Charlie and his sister, Creeping Jenny, hung from high shelves and formed screens of emerald and white leaves.

Philip changed buses and sat next to her on the way to the Mendenhall Glacier. They walked round the curve of the lake. Fireweed, known to Lilian as willow herb, grew everywhere. The Alaskans said that once its flowers turned to cotton fluff, then winter was six weeks away. The fluff was just beginning to appear. Two blue grouse, one male, one female strolled, stately and unafraid, on the path.

He asked what she usually did for dinner. She dined alone.

"Well," he smiled, "I invite you to have dinner with me tonight in the Castello. It's the small Italian restaurant. You can sit near a window and watch the sea and the lights on shore."

"All right," she said, "but I don't have any fancy clothes."

She stopped at one of the expensive shops on the

way back to her cabin and bought a long silk scarf with an abstract pattern in red and purple. She would never have paid seventy-five pounds for it in England.

She sat on her balcony, watching the evening settle over the water and wrote cards to the children. She had a mobile phone but did not want to use it; she hated the crude abbreviations of texting and found talking at a distance stilted. The children had all, led by her emphatic and stubborn daughter, taken her side in the divorce and refused to have contact with their father. Lilian had not found the strength to talk to them about the anger.

Geoff was head teacher in the secondary school where she had taught English. He had been having an affair with his deputy, a younger woman, for over two years. She should perhaps have known. Everyone else seemed to.

The Filipino steward knocked on the cabin door and came in to turn down the bedcover. He placed, on the pillow, a chocolate wrapped in gold foil, a single fuchsia and a piece of lavender paper with a motto on it in italic writing. She picked it up and read "Leap and the net will appear." She smiled and thought that nets had a lot of holes.

She put on her smartest trousers and shirt, and

looped the new scarf round her shoulders. She looked at herself in the mirror. She had kept fit and slim through walking and Pilates and a sensible diet and thought herself still attractive, with pale blue eyes and brown, grey-streaked hair, well cut.

She met Philip in the restaurant, overlooking the dark sea. An aria from *La Traviata* was playing. There were pictures of Venice on the walls. A waiter, Polish not Italian, bowed her to their table. Philip stood to greet her. He said she looked wonderful and admired the scarf. He wore a blue-and-white-striped shirt with a white collar and a cricket club tie. She thought about how she and Geoff had scoffed at men who wore this combination and had joked about how they probably also wear socks with sandals. But she was not with Geoff.

Dinner was excellent: a delicate celery soup, crisp salad and lasagne oozing with vegetables, followed by Italian cheese. Philip ordered a bottle of Chablis and they had a smooth Italian red with the cheese.

"What do you do in England?" he asked.

She told him about teaching and about Geoff.

"What a shit," he said. "That's terrible. But divorce isn't always bad. I know several people who divorced, then found someone else quite quickly. "

"What do you do?" she asked.

He had been in charge of an import/export company but had taken semi-retirement when his wife developed cancer. She had been ill for two years, having invasive treatment. The cancer spread from a lung to the brain.

"I am sorry," she said. "They say that you don't get over death, you get used to it, and I hope that will happen for you. Do you have any family?"

He had two sons, one in the US, one in Australia, aged thirty-five and thirty-three, both in banking.

He had been a local Conservative councilor and mayor in Gloucestershire and worked with a number of charities and a local children's center. He was to receive a knighthood in the New Year for his contribution to business and the voluntary sector. He may well be invited to go into the House of Lords. He admired Mrs. Thatcher and respected Tony Blair for his stance on the Iraq war. She did not say that she and Geoff and the children had marched through London in the anti-war demonstration and had left the Labour Party because of the UK intervention in Iraq.

Philip insisted that she was his guest and paid, leaving a generous tip. He took her arm to guide her from the restaurant and to her cabin. At the door, he took her hand, kissed her cheek and suggested that they meet for a drink the following evening, then have dinner again.

The ship sailed overnight to Skagway and docked at seven in the morning. Lilian had an early start for a guided walk up part of the old Chilcoot Trail, forged during the Klondike gold rush between 1897 and 1899. She had read about it in Jack London's stories. Philip was taking a guided bus tour round the town and mining areas.

In the early morning, the clouds licked the tops of the trees and the air was pearly and pine-scented. The trail was steep at first and two of the group of six were slow and ponderous. The two young men she had seen in the restaurant were on the trip and were fit and fast. The group paused at a crest on the high, damp path overlooking the Taiya River. The guide told what to do if a bear appeared. Make yourself tall and make a noise for a brown bear, play dead for a black one. She waved a mace spray to reassure them.

Curly lichens, like oyster shells, clung to the bases of trees. Exotic mushrooms, red, black and gold, grew in crevasses. They tried the low-stemmed wild

The Upside Down Trees

cranberries and grimaced at the sourness. They saw bear droppings, paw prints in the mud on the ground and scratching on the trees, but no bears.

They walked for two hours. Lilian chatted to the two young men, Simon and John, estate agents in south London. They, too were going on to the national park and invited her for a drink one evening.

A slippery path dropped down to the river. Moist sunlight now warmed the air, tinting the ripples. Lilian saw to her relief that there was very little whitewater. They put on oversized waterproof boots and scrambled onto a large, raft of thick yellow polyurethane to go downriver.

Lilian spotted two couples of bald eagles in the trees, vigilant and motionless, heads white capped, yellow upper beaks fiercely hooked over the lower. Another pair on an island were gouging the pink flesh of a salmon. The raft scuttled along in the clear, shallow water, occasionally sticking on stones, until they reached the bank where the bus driver waited to hand out hot chocolate and muffins.

On board again, Lilian showered, wishing there was a bath to ease her limbs, and dressed for dinner. She thought how pleasant it would be to see Philip that evening and tell him about the Chilcoot Trail and hear about his tour.

They went for a drink in the Glacier bar. Philip insisted on champagne. He had found the bus tour unexciting and the people fat and boring.

They dined and showed each other photographs of their families. As they looked at one of her and the children, he said, "Lilian, you are a very attractive woman. Has there been no one else since your husband left? I can't believe that some man hasn't been after you."

"No," she said. "Frankly, I haven't wanted to get involved again. How about you?"

"Well, actually," he replied, "I was having an affair before my wife was ill, and it carried on until recently. But she was married, panicked and ended it. I was very upset. I do like to have a lady around."

As they finished dinner, Philip suggested the piano bar for a drink. The trio of piano, guitar and drums were playing Frank Sinatra songs. He ordered champagne and asked her to dance. She felt awkward at being close to a man again. Philip held her tightly and her head dropped to his shoulder. After two dances, she said that she was tired and must go as they had an early start the next day.

The Upside Down Trees

He escorted her to her cabin again. He held her shoulders as he said goodnight and tried to kiss her on the lips. She turned away, thanked him for dinner and opened her door.

Lilian got into bed, and looked at the daily chocolate and flower and motto. This one said "Every journey starts with a small step." She reflected that steps should be taken on firm ground, based in reality and with a guidebook. She slept badly and dreamed of Philip, naked by a swimming pool. She woke at four, sexually aroused for the first time in two years. She masturbated to orgasm.

The ship sailed into Glacier Bay. The early mist cleared as they approached the glaciers. Over coffee, Philip said that he would try to change his travel plans so that he could carry on with the tour to Denali. She suggested that it might be very expensive. He said that it wasn't a problem and he would like to see Denali and get to know her better. She stared at the horizon.

Philip took photographs of her with the glaciers in the background. Their pale blue ridges and deeper blue recesses glistened. The sea was dark and calm, dotted with ice floes. They moved alongside Margerie Glacier, two miles wide and constantly, imperceptibly moving.

As the ship turned, a huge piece of ice calved from its bulk and cascaded into the sea.

In College Fjord, the lines of glaciers, seven on each side, were named after the American colleges attended by travelers who first discovered the area. On the left were the Ivy League colleges, and on the right the women's colleges, the seven sisters.

"How interesting," Lilian said. "I spent a year at Vassar studying American women writers after my degree."

"Good heavens," replied Philip, "I didn't know you were so clever."

Lilian did not want lunch and went to the gym for a yoga class and a massage, then back to her cabin. The steward had left two chocolates, a fuchsia and motto. This one read "Measure twice, cut once." She smiled. Geoff's father, a meticulous and wary carpenter from Yorkshire used to say this at times of indecision.

She showered and put on the only dress she had brought with her, draped the silk scarf around her and pinned it with a silver brooch.

They drank almost a bottle of champagne in the bar before dinner. In the corridor, on the way to the restaurant, he pulled her to him and kissed her on

The Upside Down Trees

the lips. He opened her mouth with his tongue and explored her. She responded with her lips and tongue and pressed against him. He pushed his erection into her belly. She pulled away and breathed deeply.

"That was nice," he said, "let's remember it."

He ordered white wine and toasted a special meal and a special person. The waiter took their orders and brought complimentary glasses of prosecco. He asked Philip if he should take a photograph "of you and your lovely lady." Lilian said no and Philip said yes at the same time.

Simon and John came in and sat at the other end of the restaurant, elegant in dark suits and bow ties.

"I see that our queer friends are here," said Philip.

"What do you mean?" she asked.

"Those two over there. Sharing a cabin, no doubt. I wonder what they get up to. I've got no time for this civil partnership business. And I hear they can even adopt now. It's disgraceful that the law can be so silly."

She was silent, not knowing how to respond, but finally said, "Simon and John are charming, kind and interesting. It doesn't matter about their sexuality."

She played with her napkin and nibbled a piece of bread, not looking at him. She felt tearful. She glanced across at Simon and John who were laughing and talking. She sat up rigidly and breathed slowly.

"My younger son, Brian, is gay. That's what he calls himself. Not queer. He has a delightful partner and they are going to have a civil ceremony next spring."

"I'm sorry," he said, patting her hand. "Can't people get counseling for that sort of thing?"

"You haven't heard me," she said. "My son is what he is, and always has been. He is happy being gay, he doesn't just accept it. He doesn't need counseling."

She thought she was going to cry. Brian had suffered some bullying at school, but only spoke about it later, and said that he would fight to protect others. When he was seventeen, he told her and Geoff that he knew he was gay, and had sobbed in her arms, whilst she stroked his hair and told him that she was proud of him.

"Let's change the subject," Philip said. "I can see you're upset, but let's not ruin the evening. Have some more wine."

She wanted to get back to her cabin and be alone. She picked at her risotto and salad but refused dessert and wine. Philip talked about his farm and business, and plans for future travel. She was silent, except to remark on the food. She said she felt faint in the heat and had to leave. He walked her to her door and, when they arrived, pointed to the floor.

"I have a surprise. Look in the ice bucket down there. It's a bottle of champagne for us to have in your cabin as it's my last night."

"I'd rather not," she said. "I feel very tired and want to disembark early tomorrow to see a bit of Seward before we get the train."

"Just one little drink," he continued. "You can throw the rest away."

They went into the cabin. He opened the champagne and poured a large amount into two beakers.

"Here's to us and the rest of your trip and to meeting again," he said.

She did not repeat this, but opened the door to go out onto the balcony. He followed her, and put his arms round her to draw her to him.

"I want to make love to you," he whispered. "Let's just finish our champagne."

She poured the champagne into the sea and pushed past him.

"What's the matter?" he asked. "We've had some great times, now you go all cold. Is it about your son? Look, I'm not a bigot. I don't really care about how other people behave."

"I'm very tired," she said, "and I need to phone my daughter."

She opened the cabin door for him.

"Oh, all right," he said. "But I'll get up early tomorrow to see you off, and we'll meet back in England. Write down your phone number and email. I'll contact you soon, and send you the photos."

She gave him the wrong phone number and the wrong email address, and planned to be off the boat as soon as it docked at five in the morning.

She found her mobile phone in the rummage of a suitcase and went onto the balcony. A hard, precise moon dabbled in the water, furrowed as the ship pushed towards Seward. It would be early morning in England, but her daughter would be awake and having her first cup of tea when the phone rang.

The Road to Napanee

by

Joanna Pocock

When they stopped to pick her up, Ray was surprised Stephanie didn't give him one of her lectures about responsibility. She never did approve of Ray's habit of taking in strays. It wasn't so much the weirdos that Stephanie disliked, it was the fact that Ray made no effort to hide his kinship to them. He felt closer to the misfits and drunks than he did to his own wife and child.

But tonight Ray was not about to drive past a woman alone on a highway in minus-thirty-degree weather, with nothing but a rucksack and a cardboard sign saying "NAPANEE." The tires skidded as he came to a stop.

Stephanie turned sharply to look at him, "What the hell?" But her question was cut short as the woman jumped in.

"Thanks," the stranger said, tucking her bag by her feet. She rubbed her hands together and blew on them.

"It's fucking cold out there."

Stephanie said, "Hey, watch it." And looked meaningfully at the small girl sleeping on her lap.

"She's out cold," Ray said in the hitchhiker's defense. "She can't hear a thing."

"Oh, sorry," the hitchhiker said.

Stephanie told the hitchhiker their names and then asked for hers.

"Karl," came the reply.

In his rear view mirror Ray noticed the dark patches under her eyes. A pretty panda, he thought.

"Karl. Isn't that a boy's name?" Stephanie had her school teacher's voice on.

"Yeah, my dad wanted a boy but all he got was me." Karl laughed.

"Oh, I see." Stephanie turned back to face the front and was about to say something else when Ray switched the radio to the one station his car could pick up. He felt Karl tapping in time to the music against the back of his seat. Snow fell softly on the road ahead. He was taking it extra slow.

"You should have got snow tires before we left. We'd be in Toronto by now if you had." Why Stephanie had to bring this up just at this moment with the beautiful fresh snow, the music, the sleeping child and the stranger in the back was beyond Ray. He glanced at Karl in the rearview mirror. She was staring out the window.

"Everyone is passing us," Stephanie added.

And it was true. Cars were zooming past.

"Well, I didn't get snow tires so that's that." Ray shot an embarrassed smile at Karl who gave him a startled look in return, as if she knew more than he did.

"Don't you just love all this snow?" Karl said. "It's so clean and quiet. It covers up all the shit everywhere. It even makes Napanee look pretty."

"Is that where you're from then?" Stephanie still faced forward, shifting Emily on her lap. Ray thought four was too old to be sleeping on your mother's lap, not to mention the safety issue. Forget snow tires, if they were in an accident Emily's little body would be flung around like a rag doll.

"Yup. Napanee," Karl replied wearily. Then out came a productive, chesty cough. With one hand shielding Emily's face, Stephanie gave Ray a do-you-think-it's-contagious look. The little girl carried on peacefully in a very deep sleep.

The hitchhiker recovered her voice. "You wouldn't think so, but even a town as small as Napanee gets dirty. You find shit all over the place when the snow melts." Karl cleared her throat again. "Even my dad's toenails got dirt under them. The guy never even went outside. But when I used to cut them I couldn't believe how much was crusted in there."

Ray spotted a gas station up ahead, its lights shining through the early dusk. "How 'bout a coffee?" He said with exaggerated uplift. What he was really gasping for was a drink, but he'd been dry for a month now and with Christmas coming he was trying hard. Colored lights flashed around the windows splattered with fake snow. He turned the radio off and stopped the car.

"So anyone for coffee?" he repeated.

"No thanks. It'll come in one of those Styrofoam cups. Do you know that those plastic cups are giving us all cancer? The chemicals from them have been found in the breast milk of polar bears. Those cups and the people who drink from them are killing polar bears and everything else on this fucking planet."

Ray pretended to ignore Karl. Opening his door a crack, he turned to his wife. "Anything for you Steph?"

She looked out over the dashboard and Ray recognized her calorie-counting expression.

"A hot chocolate with marshmallows, if they've got

any. And an apple juice for Emily."

He asked Karl one more time if she wanted anything, and she shook her head. Ray stepped out, and before shutting the door he leaned in and asked Stephanie if she'd be okay.

"Fine," she said. "I need to pee though. So be quick."

Ray crossed the forecourt and while he was paying he looked back at the car. The windows were fogged up and all he could make out were the fuzzy outlines of the two women. They looked like dolls. Not moving, just sitting. Stephanie was probably worrying about pneumonia, TB, or the imagined dagger in Karl's sock. She excelled at imagining catastrophes which disappointed her by never occurring. He wondered what Karl saw, whether she could make out the shreds of what they had, or if it was too late to see even those.

As he approached the car both women looked at him. Stephanie said she was going for her pee. She slipped Emily from her lap and got out of the car. "If she wakes up can you give her some juice?" she asked Ray.

"Yup, sure thing." He knew he was sounding lighter and brighter for the sake of the stranger. He then offered Karl a butter tart, which she refused.

"They came free with the coffee. Christmas cheer

and all that." He held up the bag printed with red, white and green snowmen.

"You know they're poisoning us with all that refined sugar."

"Who's they?" Ray asked.

"Oh, you know, the bankers, large companies, corporations, all those fat cats taking advantage of us little people."

"What have they got to do with sugar?"

"Oh, it's all linked. Nobody sees it though. Well not people like you." Karl was fired up and suddenly took on the expression of a zealot. "You see if you get everyone hooked on sugar and make them fat then they can't do anything. They sit all day watching TV and hey presto you have an instant audience you can beam your advertising to. Oh what the fuck. You would never understand."

She was right. Ray didn't have a clue what she was on about. He wanted to ask her if she was one of those conspiracy theorists but Stephanie was already back.

She awkwardly maneuvered herself into the car placing Emily's little body onto her lap. "What are those?" she asked pointing to the bag on Ray's knee.

"Butter tarts," Ray said. He looked nervously at

Karl who was blankly staring out at the forecourt.

"May I?" Stephanie asked.

Ray stuck the bag on the dashboard, "Help yourself."

Stephanie took a bite, and bits of pastry fell onto Emily's hair. Ray reached over to brush them off.

"So have you two been married long?" The question came at the couple after another fit of coughing. Karl's lips were unnaturally red and thin, and her pale face and large grey eyes made Ray think of the pre-Raphaelite poster Stephanie had up in her bedroom when they first met.

"Almost five years," Stephanie said. Ray stared at his daughter's chest rising and falling and her face unmarked by worry.

Karl continued, "I don't get to meet too many married people. So what's the deal? Are you guys happy?" Ray was wishing he were sitting across a table from her talking through the merits of single life. A cigarette. A beer. A dance. And a hand on a hip.

"That's a funny question! I don't know. Ray what do you say? Are we happy?" Stephanie was trying to sound light as if she were teasing him.

He reached into the bag of butter tarts. "Of course

we are honey. I wouldn't be here if I weren't happy."

"There, does that answer your question?" Stephanie seemed satisfied that this conversation was coming to an end.

"Sort of. I mean the only people I know who have stuck together went past the happy stage into something else, like a sort of zombie stage. My folks didn't though. My mom up and left when I was five. I don't hate her for it. She just was never meant to have kids. Some people shouldn't."

Stephanie blew on her hot chocolate. Ray wanted to know about Karl's mother but Stephanie got in there and asked if she had any plans to get married.

"Are you crazy?" A hoarse high laugh erupted.

"Why's that then?" Stephanie asked.

"It's like sugar. It's just another way of getting people where you want them. Of keeping them in check. No way José. Not for me. I want to be free. No sugar in my bowl."

Stephanie looked at Ray, "Sugar?"

"Yeah, don't worry about it. Karl and I had a little chat about sugar while you were in the john."

Stephanie tapped Ray on the thigh and frowned. It was her code to let him know she was worried. He ignored her and sipped his coffee. He wanted to get going again but Emily began to stir.

"I'm thirsty," a tired voice rose from Stephanie's lap.

Stephanie got the apple juice out. "Ray I'm going to have to put Emily in the back seat. She's getting too heavy." She looked at him meaningfully.

"Okay," he said, oblivious.

"But do you think it is okay with all that coughing?" Stephanie lowered her voice for the last word and, angling her head towards the back seat, she looked hard at Ray.

"Oh that. Yeah, it'll be fine," he said, glancing in the mirror at Karl to see if she had clocked his wife's comment. A pair of grey heavy-lashed eyes looked back at him knowingly. He wanted to say sorry to those eyes.

"C'mon honey, in the back you go." Stephanie twisted around and helped Emily through the two front seats. "Now here's your juice."

"No." Emily squirmed and held onto her mother.

"But there isn't enough room up here. And you can't sit on mommy's lap all the way home. It's illegal. Now in the back you go." Stephanie unhooked Emily's chubby hands from her arm and eventually got the girl sitting in her car seat with her pink blanket.

Karl stared out the window ignoring the little girl next to her.

"Mommy," Emily wailed.

"Emily, you're alright. Now drink your juice." Stephanie handed her the small square box with its straw poking out. The girl knocked it to the floor.

The wailing continued. It soon became crying.

Over the noise Ray said, "Stephanie, why don't you go sit with her?" He would have suggested anything for some peace and quiet.

Stephanie shot him an angry glance. "Oh all right then." The two women got out of the car and swapped places.

It seemed to Ray that Karl was looking a bit smug. She took off her jacket to put her seatbelt on, and at that moment he caught a breath of her scent. It reminded him of the smell that came up from the ground when he raked the leaves in the fall. Earth and sun and just enough decay to start making life again.

"Karl can you pass me my hot chocolate?" There was a touch of anger in Stephanie's voice. "And the butter tarts."

Ray knew that later on he'd get the blame for making her go over her allotted number of calories for the day. The fat on her hips would be his fault.

Karl turned towards Stephanie, the leather jacket on her lap making a crisp twisting sound, and handed her the bag and the hot chocolate.

"So are we ready?" Ray took a final sip of coffee and put it back into the mug holder on the dashboard. He glanced at Karl's legs and noticed her jeans were worn over her knees. They looked bonier than he would have liked.

He cranked up the radio, and sang along to "After the Fire is Gone."

"It's crazy isn't it? I mean this is why two people should never get together in the first place. Tammy Wynette, Patsy Cline, and all the rest of them, they knew a thing or two." Karl had a renewed confidence about her and shook her head with emphasis as she spoke. He snatched a look out of the corner of his eye. She had a surprisingly fine profile.

Stephanie spoke over the singing. "I can't hear anything you two are saying with that music blaring away up there."

"We weren't saying anything," Ray said, brusquely turning the radio down. He let out an exasperated sigh. Karl looked over at him and smiled. He hoped

Stephanie hadn't seen. God she was pretty. If only he'd listened to Stephanie and gone up north on his own this weekend, he'd be alone with this girl. For once he had convinced Stephanie to shield him from his crazy family and it had completely backfired.

With Karl sitting next to him, he felt he had committed some crime, when all he had wanted was for Emily to stop crying. He tried to catch Stephanie's eye in the mirror but she was staring hard at the hills of snow, which had become simple outlines in the dusk. He couldn't see his daughter but imagined she was now happily sipping her juice next to her mother, his wife.

ぐ

After an hour or so of driving they arrived in Napanee. The snowplow hadn't passed through, and there was waist-high snow on the roads. The car crept through the center of town, keeping to the tracks made by the wheels of previous vehicles.

Then Emily piped up. "Have you got a best friend?"

Karl was taken by surprise. "Um, yeah, I guess so."

"My best friend is Freya." Emily said. "She broke her arm and went to the hospital."

The Road to Napanee

Ray intervened. "Honey, I don't think Karl needs to hear about Freya."

"Ray, don't get angry. It's not like she's doing anything wrong," Stephanie argued.

"I know, it's just that… ," Ray didn't know what it was exactly. Was he embarrassed at the mundanity of his child? What seemed to him her pointless preoccupations.

"Anywhere here is fine," Karl said as they drove through the quiet streets.

Ray thought Karl sounded sad, but he often heard things that weren't there.

"Will you be alright? Everything looks pretty closed." He strained to see out the iced-up windows.

"Yup. Fine. I've got a room with a friend just over there." Karl cleared her throat and pointed at a squat red brick building.

"Can we go into your house?" Emily asked.

"No, honey I don't think so," Stephanie said.

Karl held her hand out for Ray to shake. "Well, it was nice meeting you."

Ray shook her hand, feeling the fragile bones. Her skin was warm and softer than he expected. She turned to Stephanie, who was explaining to Emily why you can't invite yourself into strange people's houses.

"You can have your seat back now," Karl said as she undid her seatbelt.

She got out of the car and pulled her leather jacket tight around her thin body. Stephanie was busy reasoning with Emily about going into the front seat without having her on her lap while Karl walked around to the driver's side. She leaned into the open window. Ray was convinced she was going to kiss him.

"Don't go listening to too many of those bleeding heart songs. They're not good for your health. And stay away from sugar. It'll kill you." She smiled and he saw her teeth for the first time. They were small and square like a child's.

Stephanie was now in the passenger seat doing an exaggerated shiver. "God it's freezing."

Karl stepped aside and Ray pulled the car away from where she was standing. He put his arm out the window and waved.

"God, what a weirdo!" Stephanie pushed the buttons on the radio until she came to a phone-in show. She turned up the volume and Ray felt her hand on his thigh.

"How about dinner. Are you hungry yet?" Her voice had gone from school teacher to wife almost instantly.

"I guess I could eat. We'll stop at the next town."

Ray was back on the highway, driving through the darkness. On the radio a woman was talking about the belly dancing classes she'd taken to lose weight, spice up her sex life and make her more confident. They worked so well, she ended up dumping her husband, leaving her children, and marrying the teacher. Ray could imagine what she looked like just from the voice. It surprised him how much he hated this woman. He wanted to smash her face. Then he hated himself for thinking like this. The radio audience clapped and Stephanie laughed.

"Imagine that."

"What mommy?"

Ray sped up, wishing he'd paid the extra for snow tires. Stephanie was explaining to Emily the difference between belly dancing and ballet dancing and Ray caught a glimpse of his daughter nodding sagely at this information. He couldn't wait to get to the next town and out of the car and away from that radio and all those voices. He closed his eyes for a split second and swore he could smell that earthy scent. There was no snow at all for that second, just grass and leaves, a long, fine fall evening and the beginning of something new, something like life.

Joanna Pocock

Snail Honey

by

Travis Dahlke

"This is what we're doing. We are going to the beach, and we're gonna make a big sandcastle," says the guy with a neck beard and Orlando Magic sweatpants.

Tortilla chips, soft with guacamole run-off, spill from my mouth.

"How big?" I ask, half crying.

Neckbeard makes a gesture with his hands that indicates approximately two feet.

"No, no we're not doing that," I say.

Dueling flamenco guitar solos wail over maracas and a trumpet, somewhere in the background. Neckbeard looks around the cantina and asks me where all the cactus paintings are. I tell him something about democracy and it's all over.

Earlier, we had been selling Snail Honey in Arkansas. Except Neckbeard called it "our Kansas," and I decided quickly not to correct him. We sold the honey for eight dollars a jar. Before being emptied, these jars had originally been used for pine nuts, which are an expensive nut. Not eight-dollars-a-jar expensive, but pricey. They were stolen anyway. Unlike nuts, honey is a type of sticky, amber liquid used for heightening the experience of chicken nuggets and sweetening tea, among other things. Before it's bottled in pine nut jars, the honey is extracted from beehives and diluted with citric acid. At about this time, a customer would furrow their brow and ask: "Where exactly does the snail come in?" And I would then explain all about how it's really extracted from boiled fair-trade snail shells and naturally fermented with pomegranate for a bone-fortifying, amino-B4-enriched, finished product. We don't tell the customers that it actually comes from a BPA-infested plastic bottle shaped like a bear, prior to being sealed in old pine nut jars. Just a minor detail we choose to omit.

Life was hard on the road for my compadres and I. Our '97 Chevy Express was full to the brim with boxes of Snail Honey, and I couldn't tell if the rattling sound above 65 mph was the jars clanking together or the catalytic converter trying to fall off. But I would say that the thick of our adventure started on a day in a desert where there used to be a cornfield.

Travis Dahlke

"I think there used to be cornfield here." I tell this to Dr. Billclinton, and I suspect Neckbeard hears, too. Dr. Billclinton is an agrologist. This means she specializes in studying grass. She studies seeds, lawns, fields, fronds, you name it. Professionally, she does it to further advance the technology of lawn care and maintenance. Suburban agriculture and whatnot. Personally, she just loves how encompassing and important grass is to mankind, or something to that regard. I don't say this out loud, but I do believe I am in love with her. Before all of this, I had big plans for the Australian countryside. I was gonna go there and marry some tough broad to live in a shack and raise dingoes or grow pumpkins with miscellaneous vegetation. I told acquaintances that I didn't really care how tough the soil is in the outback. And they would tell me that there's more to that country than outbacks and dingoes. There is more to life than outbacks and dingoes. (Yeah, right). But then Dr. Billclinton enters my life. An agrologist from some podunk town in Australia. My dream lady. Right from between the lines of my Christmas list to the Aboriginal gods.

The three of us stand inside the entrance of an Arizonian diner. This waitress with a "Halle" name tag semi-politely informs us that we can seat ourselves. Neckbeard sits next to Dr. Billclinton in the booth and I get my own little area. Dr. Billclinton plays with the duct tape on the vinyl while I thumb through the tabletop jukebox selection. Neckbeard asks if they have any Batch.

"It's pronounced Bok," I tell him.

"What did I say?" Neckbeard mutters, but he's transfixed on the menu. I know I'm getting buttermilk pancakes, but I look at the menu anyway, seeing as how the jukebox was just for show and the buttons don't even depress. Outside the window, the sun is white and wavy, just the way I like it. The greenhouse effect is in full swing, with heat breathing in through the glass. The three of us are baking inside of a stainless steel, bolts-and-vinyl satellite nestled on a squishy parking lot. Bear grass jutting out from the cracks. The waitress makes her way to our booth and pours instant coffee into shiny brown mugs. I can tell from the dusty odor.

"Do you have anyone to soilate the xerophyllym in the parking lot?" Dr. Billclinton suddenly asks Halle. Halle is fifty-eight or an unhealthy forty-five. She smells like tobacco and the color mauve. Her uniform matches the picture of the French toast sundae on the very last page of the menu.

I grunt a polite chuckle so that the waitress will feel less uncomfortable. "Excuse me. The bear grass. It's a predatory perennial to the fig population."

"The plants are a threat to the bugs?" Halle says. She does not look pleased. Dr. Billclinton gives Halle her menu.

"Figs aren't insects. They're a breed of sparrow," Dr. Billclinton tells her. Even I didn't know that. Food is delivered on slippery plates and napkins are scrunched up into little balls. The doctor offers to pay and lets us know that she'll meet us outside.

I am picking at pieces of pancake in my molar outside the diner. Neckbeard is asking the doctor about her necklace, and she makes up a story about her grandmother passing it down through the generations because she made it through some historic blimp fire in the 1930s. I stop and pivot on my heels.

"Hold on. My doggy bag." I start to head back into the diner but Dr. Billclinton throws her arm against my chest and tells me to leave it.

"I have a whole second meal of pancakes in there," I plead.

"You have nothing in there," she tells me. "And you

Snail Honey

don't really need all that refined sugar," she says jabbing my stomach, in a low voice. This gets a laugh out of Neckbeard, even though he is at least thirty pounds overweight and should absolutely not be chuckling at my expense. I abandon my pancakes and follow my compadres into the van. Forward on an aimless adventure to peddle snake oil. To this day I cannot eat pancakes. I should've known then that something wasn't right, but sugar and sunlight can make a man mighty numb to the sound of sirens.

The sun sets and rises a few times, and some celebrity scandals entertain the three of us on motel TVs with rusty rabbit ears. These big, navy blue storm clouds form in our wake, but we point the van towards sun. We've clocked 300 miles on the odometer. Driving to some town the doctor promises will be a lucrative venture. The check-engine light has come on and I am less than optimistic about passing emissions.

"Not in Arizona," Dr. Billclinton tells me. She's driving. She sits too close to the dashboard, and her pale arms look awkward at the steering wheel. "They don't do emission testing out here. It's like the Wild West of automotive pollution." Neckbeard is asleep in the back. We bought the van, used, from a car lot at three in the morning. No salesmen necessary, but we left some stock certificates in its place. They were really just pieces of construction paper that Neckbeard drew dollar signs on with forged "Winston Churchill" signatures. Okay, we stole it.

There were three cassette tapes that came with the van, under the front passenger's seat. Dr. Billclinton snapped the radio antennae off and used it to toast marshmallows over a small brushfire we made one night. But hey, no radio, no problem. I ask her if we're there yet, and instead of laughing she says: "That's funny."

She rolls down the window and the wind whips at her ponytail. I try to fall asleep in my seat with fabric that smells like Sprite. I imagine Dr. Billclinton and I holding hands while riding cartoon koalas underwater. I try to imagine her without a ponytail and glasses but it's difficult and the ocean tastes far too much like soda.

"Lawrence, wake up!" Neckbeard is shaking me. "We're here!"

"In-where-in?" I say with closed eyes. My nose is unbelievably itchy. I can hear Dr. Billclinton unloading crates of Snail Honey from the back of the van.

"Welcome to Greenlee," the doctor exclaims with open arms. The first thing I notice about Greenlee is the

Snail Honey

air. It's obnoxiously fresh, as if located in the eye of a pine forest storm. But all I can make out is commerce. Chains and gas stations. Lots of brown metal traffic signs.

"Look." Neckbeard points to the distance. "Incredible," he whispers like a child seeing an actual triceratops pissing in his front yard. I have never seen so many houses, the same color, so close together. Miles of them in the distance. Off-white siding and red ceramic roof tiles. They're nestled on a giant hill that seems to wind down forever. A waterfall of suburbs swirling and cascading in a perfect Fibonacci spiral. Neckbeard tells me he wants to live there someday. The distant sparkles of above-ground swimming pools are blinding as my eyeballs struggle to focus. The doctor hands me a crate. She leads Neckbeard and I around the front of a building into a vacant, grassy lot.

"Astroturf," she says. She puts her finger in her mouth like she's trying to gag.

"What's with all the lemonade stands?" Neckbeard inquires.

"It's the Greenlee Sunday Farmer's Market," Dr. Billclinton tells us. And it is indeed. Fresh tomatoes, corn, pesto, bread, and fish. Organic soaps, pie, carrots, beef and tea. Parents with sweater ponchos and kids on leashes. Kids with labs on leashes. Old senile people with orange skin and white hair. Single thirty-somethings slurping iced chai from green straws.

"Everyone's wearing hats," Neckbeard frowns. The three of us stand side by side. Our hand-painted sign is a banner flying over some samples that we spread out on a picnic blanket with a grass stain that the doctor covered up with a ceramic snail. Some old lady with sunglasses covering her entire face shuffles up. I can feel Neckbeard's fear and uncertainty.

"Good morning," Dr. Billclinton says in her most enthusiastic voice. The old lady asks about the honey and I tell her all about it. I tell her what the doctor told me, some time ago at a truck stop four hundred miles away.

Neckbeard and I were on a reverse road trip back from a potential contracting job in New Mexico, or Old Mexico or one of the Mexicos. Needless to say, we were unqualified and were drowning our sorrows with soft drinks in a parking lot when this girl asks us if our truck needs a jump-start. She's got this razor-sharp ponytail and thick glasses frames with thin lenses. She's short but she stands with her arms on the hips of her khaki shorts in this weird power stance that makes her look taller. I tell her we don't need a jump-start and she asks our names, and I am thinking holy crap.

The part where she said we needed a bigger car to sell the Snail Honey comes after the part where she told us about how much money there was to be made from Snail Honey. She had a pen that said "Flagstaff Sheriff's Department" on it in gold. We're sitting at a picnic table, or a booth or something and she grabs this napkin and writes: "White People + Influx of jobs in South West Arizona + Farmers Markets + Pomegranate + Fair-trade ++ and Organic = $$$." And a smiley face. Except she draws the smiley face on the top of my hand. And I can feel the ball of the pen gliding on my skin and her eyes meet mine and I am like holy crap.

I watch Dr. Billclinton take a twenty-dollar bill from this old lady. The doctor says thank you with this crazy smile that makes her look like a crazy person. She does this at least forty or fifty more times that day. Neckbeard sits in a folding chair and just kind of takes it all in, until the sky gets all pink and gold. We start to pack up and when I lift the cigar box it weighs about as much as a coffee table book about canyons. We're back in the van and we're laughing and listening to the cassette deck. I'm driving while Neckbeard is in the front seat. The doctor is counting money in the back and singing along to the song. It's something about the fourth of July and for a moment I get this feeling like we're a family. Mr. and Mrs. Billclinton hyphenated with my last name, because I consider myself a progressively mobile gentleman.

"There!" The doctor points to an Applebee's. We eat apple crisp sundaes for dinner and they come out on a big, hot iron skillet. I look around at all the other families and office workers and we are no different. I see the doctor's grin through the bottom of my oversized mug and for a second it looks like she's missing a tooth. I tell her she looks familiar. Like a face from the past. But I am drunk and I tell her this in a way where all the words are connected.

"I got the bill. You guys get the van started," she says. Outside, the smoke from the vents smells like peppers and I have cinnamon from the apple crisp on my tongue. We pull out of the parking lot, right on red, and I have no idea where we are going, but I don't care. Neckbeard is asleep in the back and the doctor's driving. Three cop cars and an ambulance with blaring Christmas light sirens speed by us. We enjoy this perfect calm, and I think about the future and the cigar box getting heavier and having to buy more cigar boxes.

All the white, green and blue lights from bars and gas stations dance on the smudged-up windshield glass. It's cold tonight and the heat is on. I can smell the engine oil. The fumes stay in my nasal cavities even as we step outside in front of a motel. Big electric white sign that says "Free Ca le." I tell the doctor to inquire about the complimentary lettuce at the front desk, so that she knows I'm witty.

Neckbeard falls asleep again fast on a cot and quilt the doctor discovers in the closet. I'm lying in the twin-sized bed when Dr. Billclinton comes out of the bathroom wearing only her shorts and the same facial expression she has when she counts money. When she slides into the bed and doesn't use a pillow as a barricade I think something is going to happen and it sobers me up all too quickly. She takes my hand and she just kind of talks in these exhaled words without tone or treble. I don't talk, but I listen so close that the sound of the TV completely falls away.

"Back in, in Australia. The Milky Way would seem closer because of the difference in hemispheres. At night I used to lay outside with the lemon grass as my mattress and trace the path of the galaxy with my finger. I'd always stop and look at my palm and the infinite space beyond it. Just this contrast between my knuckles and wrist and this organic human hand thing being close, right in front of my face. And then this massive, purple painting right behind it, in this strange relationship. This contrast between hand and everything else that is utterly untouchable. I would just stay out there until dew saturated the ground." She stops and turns her head on the dusty pillow. "Someday, we're going to have a farm there. We're going to raise dingoes and have pumpkins as pets."

"What do pumpkins eat?" I croak, trying desperately not to wake up Neckbeard. Just in case. I think about trying to kiss her face, but I hesitate.

"It's Atalanta. My name," she says, before falling asleep.

"Goodnight, Atalanta."

For such a cold night, the morning air is a stagnant eighty-two degrees. I ask the doctor if the Snail Honey needs to be kept cold, and she says it's fine and to just get in the van. Neckbeard lets out a huge yawn and Dr. Billclinton blesses him. She tells him this story about how back home the old folks used to say "God bless you" when people yawned because Tasmanian phantoms would drown you in the ocean if your yawn wasn't properly blessed. Neckbeard doesn't believe her, but he draws a picture of the van on a map he finds in the glove box.

And so we go. Our van full of Snail Honey, speeding down interstates, being chased by a billowing trail of black air. Farmers market after farmers market after motel after farmers market. I cannot believe the variety of melons, let alone the squash. Don't even get me started on the squash. We make enough money to get some wicker baskets for country-chic product placement. We're halfway across Oklahoma when we've made enough money to buy new clothes. Dr. Billclinton gets this shirt with the silhouette of a bear on it and I buy the kind of hat a fisherman would wear (minus the tackle). We take a sharp right in Arkansas, when we get to an accident and there's a roadblock.

"It's muggy today," I say to the doctor. We're at our booth, and we've made enough money for a professional sign. We pack up and pile into the van for what feels like the thirtieth time. We've all memorized the words to the songs on the cassette tapes, and we've gotten tired of singing them. It never occurs to me to buy new tapes, but we've made enough money —

"— to buy a gun," Dr. Billclinton states.

Travis Dahlke   *161*

"We don't need a gun. Why do we need a gun?" I ask her.

"Fine, no gun," she says, immediately turning away. We're loading crates of Snail Honey into the van. We've mastered the skill of pouring bottles of generic-brand honey into pine nut jars. We've even made enough money to print off expensive looking labels at Staples. Complete with the image of a farm and a bunch of words like "tradition" and "superfood."

I think we're in Texas. Our booth is the fanciest of all the booths, and there have got to be at least forty or fifty other vendors here. Neckbeard says it's like the Mall of America of farmer's markets. We're adjacent to another honey stand and Neckbeard flips them off, but I slap his hand down before anyone can see. These two young guys in tight polyester walk up to the stand. The one wearing sunglasses picks up a pamphlet.

"Snails, eh?" one says to the other. I start to tell them about the antioxidants and how it helps regenerate cells that are absolutely vital for muscle growth.

"Does she come with the honey?" The guy without sunglasses says, looking at Dr. Billclinton's chest. She folds her arms and asks if they would be interested in reversing the dangerous effects of air pollution.

"It's all in this little jar of miracles," she recites.

"How does it taste?" One of the guys folds his arms too, so that his forearm muscles bulge. "What if I buy a whole case, would you want to come hang out for a while?" The other one laughs, somehow without smiling.

"Thank you, gentlemen," she says through clenched teeth. "Have a good day."

"Oh, I think you misheard him," sunglasses says, breathing more heavily. He rests his hands on the desk of the booth, wrinkling our tablecloth. "We are just two, cordial young southern gentlemen asking your patchouli ass to take a brief lunch break."

"Thank you," she says, and I can hear tears stab her voice. I want to do something brave, but I freeze up, even as I can feel hot adrenaline in my teeth. Neckbeard is sitting in his chair, silent and terrified.

"Fuck her and her fat hillbilly fuck-buddies. Let's grab the squash for G-rod and hit the beach." Sunglasses swipes up a jar of Snail Honey and they walk away. I can't look at the doctor. I tell her that I was going to fight them off but I know she doesn't believe me. She walks away and I get this feeling like she's never coming back. I think about how much I would miss her as she disappears into the parking lot.

We're driving down the Texas coastline in the Chevy Express. Dr. Billclinton tells me we're not stopping until we get to the southern-most tip of Mexico. We start keeping the money in the empty Snail Honey crates. Big wads of cash held together with the infinite supply of hair elastics in the doctor's pocket. I am beginning to think her ponytail is permanent. Sometimes when I'm driving down an endless stretch of interstate and I hear the song "A Whole New World" from the kid's movie cassette tape, I think of this one time when the doctor's glasses slid down her nose and I saw her eyes. These crazy eyes that looked like iguana scales, outlined in this crusty, black warrior paint. Literally. We made enough money to buy a novelty tin of warrior face paint. At that moment there was nothing separating her eyes from mine and I grin this massive grin when I think of this.

We make enough money to buy suits, briefcases and duffel bags. We sell twelve crates of Snail Honey to an organic grocery chain. We've made too much money and Neckbeard is crowded in the backseat with boxes full of cash that he uses as a pillow.

The three of us are driving, listening to a song without drums, about California. Neckbeard says:

"You know, this is just like that show. Two guys a girl and a pizza pl — "

I feel the bottom of the van drop out, and Neckbeard's head slams into the roof. The doctor jerks the wheel towards the shoulder, and I see thick sparks and dust in the rearview mirror. I ask Neckbeard if he's alright, as Dr. Billclinton jumps from the van. I start to inspect the damage, swatting smoke plumes with my hand. A smell of burning plastic.

"We're fucking out of here," she hurls a duffel bag into my chest.

"What?"

This guy behind us is on his car phone. He asks if we're okay, and says the entire muffler just fell off our van.

"Let's go," the doctor orders. It's starting to rain. I notice it's the first time I've seen rain in weeks. The clouds. I saw the clouds. Big dark ones, but they were behind us the whole time. Neckbeard looks up at the sky, the way a child would to catch rain. We walk off the exit, duffel bags slung over our backs. Away from a lonely, burning Chevy van slumped on the shoulder. Abandoned in the rain.

When we get to the cantina and sit down at the bar, the Doctor tells me to order her a green margarita while she heads for the door marked "Senoritas." I make the observation that this is the first time I have seen her drink. She had always said alcohol makes everything too pragmatical, whatever that means. I slide the duffel bags under our barstools, take a good look around and make sure none of these patrons are eyeing our luggage.

"I don't know what we're doing," I say to Neckbeard, stuffing the free tortilla chips into my mouth.

I glance up from the salsa and I see her. Pretty as she was that time her glasses slid down her face. Except now her hair isn't in a ponytail and she's on TV. Halle is on TV. Out of uniform, smiling in a Christmas sweater next to a guy wearing a US Navy hat. The guys from the market are on the screen. Graduation gowns on. Other people. There's a cop. Her hair is a different color. There's a phone number. All I can hear is Tex-Mex music.

I think of us lying in the motel bed. I think of all the times, talking in the van. That first time, when I told her about my Australian aspirations and she said: "No way, I grew up there!" This big surprised smile on her face. She told me she had lost her accent. The TV goes to commercial and Neckbeard tells me about sandcastles. I tell him something about democracy and

Snail Honey

the back of my throat hurts from swallowing sobs.

Dr. Atalanta Billclinton joins me at the bar. I ask her why she had to kill that waitress. Ask if she was planning on killing us, too. She pauses before withdrawing a sip of margarita.

"Larry, you don't get this wealthy paying bills and tipping the help." She takes another sip, but avoids the salt. I see this from the corner of my eye; at first I can't make my head turn to see her. "You think stealing vans and getting rich off of innocent people is right? You think that sucking off the grid and getting some slave desk job just to pay off the government is any way to live?" Her voice sounds disconnected and bitter, but I can still see that beautiful grass scientist squinting in the sun by a former cornfield.

"We never even got to the part with the hot tubs, and the Toccata-sampled rap song crescendo. The orange soil of the outback and the single-engine airplane," I say, but I don't really know what I mean. I pick up two out of three duffel bags. People in the bar are eyeing us now. Mumbling to each other about that girl from TV. The one from the rich family who went crazy.

"Come on," I say to Neckbeard. The doctor gives me this little nod, and in that moment I'll say that I became much too acquainted with the notions of possibility and redemption. But the moment passes and we just leave those ends loose.

The two of us are walking in spit rain, with thousands of dollars stuffed in gym bags. Neckbeard tells me that he knew what she was doing, and I immediately forgive him. He says he knew how much I liked her.

"Do you think she liked me?" I ask him. The duffel bag is getting heavy fast, and my arm is getting tired.

"I don't know," Neckbeard tells me.

Tex-Mex music stuck in my head. Grass scientists. Dingoes driving vans singing along with the soundtrack to *Aladdin*. An infinite variety of squash floating up into the Milky Way galaxy. Check-engine lights trying to warn me of something obvious. Waitresses and kids with grieving families. Apples on a hot skillet. Big piles of pine nuts, discarded. Stuck in my head.

"I don't know," I say.

Snail Honey

Victor and Pamina

by

Erika Jung

Victor y Pamina

Pamina arrived in late February, well after Valentine's Day. She had survived the five-hour flight from Stockholm to Madrid in a fitted white dress and glided into the terminal as a swan, feathery and blonde, above the thunder of rolling luggage.

Victor had already been waiting several hours when Pamina's plane landed. He had borrowed his roommate's car to make the six-hour journey to Madrid to pick her up. He had skipped work, which was unusual, and missed his introductory marketing class, which was not unusual.

A week earlier, walking hand-in-hand in La Plaza de Armas, Victor had mentioned to me that a friend was coming. She had entered a serious depression. She needed help and a place to stay. She was like a sister to him.

But the truth is that she was not his sister; she

was his ex-*novia*, and I will not insult my reader by bothering to translate. What could I say? *Pobrecita*.

I didn't meet Pamina until later that night, after Victor had brought her back to his apartment in Seville. I knocked on the door at 22:00, *la hora de siempre*, having eaten a too-large meal with my host family, having walked the short and rainy walk to 5 Pino de la Virgen. Victor's roommate answered and laughed upon seeing me.

Bueno, la otra rubia ha llegado!

"So, the other blonde has arrived!" He warned me not to go upstairs, that I would not like what I would find there.

Los cigarillos

The night we met, Victor offered me a cigarette. Pamina was still in Sweden at that time; she and Victor hadn't spoken in months.

Solamente tabaco? I asked, pointing to the cigarette, *o algo más interesante*? I don't touch tobacco. *Yo tampoco, de verdad*, he said to me as he lit up. Only *de vez en cuando*. It was a contradiction, the first of many. He smoked, but he was not a smoker. Just once in a while, at night, with friends.

(After a beer.

While driving.

After meals.

Whenever he needed it.)

Hours later, his fingers still tasted like ash. The powdery smoke remained in the ridges of his fingerprints, soft pads turned bitter in my mouth.

Afterwards, he sat on the edge of the bed with his elbows on his knees and digested another cigarette in long, slow drags. He asked me if I had ever smoked before, and why not, and wasn't I curious. There were many things I had never done before.

I told him *de verdad* about my older sister who is the way she is because our mother smoked while pregnant but doesn't anymore. I asked him if he had ever tried to quit, if he ever worried. *Bueno*, he said, *hay muchos padres fumadores*, emptying himself of white smoke.

La Esperanza de Triana

Carmen and Paco were my host parents. They lived with their adopted daughter and granddaughter, Veronica and Bea, in a small apartment above a Chinese buffet on a street called La Esperanza de Triana in a neighborhood famous for its gypsies.

They had hosted international students continuously for the past fifteen years, and my *señora* frequently talked about her previous houseguests. Laura, who was quite wealthy. Abigail, who was very shy. Elizabeth, who was spoiled rotten. Felicity, who ran every day. Michael, who was a boy. Stephanie, who was treacherous. I wondered what my epithet would be, what Carmen would tell her next guests about me.

There were three bedrooms. Veronica and Bea shared a room and a bed. Cha-Cha and I shared a room so small I could have reached out in my sleep and touched her. Carmen and Paco shared a bed in the master bedroom, although Paco almost never slept there at night.

There was a kitchen which technically I wasn't allowed to enter since my *señora* was territorial about such things.

There was one bathroom for the six of us, and hot water was available between 7:00 and 10:00.

El puente

It was called El Puente de San Telmo, and it crossed El Río Guadalquivir. I lived to the east of the river, in Triana, and had to cross it every day in order to reach the university. At night, the bridge became resplendent.

My *señora* claimed that El Río Guadalquivir was among the most contaminated bodies of water in Europe, but I had seen dogs and children swimming there. The water was dark and reflective.

The night we met, Victor and I crossed the bridge together side by side. I was on the right, between Victor and the road. He was on the left, between me and the shoulder-high guard rail. I could tell he was embarrassed when he asked to switch sides. I realized he was afraid of the height, afraid of the water below.

No puedes nadar? Couldn't he swim? He replied that he could, but that he did not trust what he could not see.

Below, a silhouette in a canoe was paddling homeward.

Lección de inglés

Y por qué coño no me enseñas algo de tu idioma? Once a month or so, always as if it were a completely novel idea, Victor would ask me. He desperately wanted to learn English, and he knew I could teach him. He already possessed a few words, high-school vocabulary from Catholic private school in Medellín.

"You know why he wants to learn English, right?" Pamina challenged from the other side of the small, wire table of *el café de siempre*. Her legs were crossed, and she had taken off her *zapatos de tacón* in order to massage her blistered left foot. A cigarette smoldered in the ashtray.

To practice on me, to understand my culture, to seduce all the *rubias* of the world, the authentic blonde Americans who came to Spain but knew no Spanish.

But Victor did not speak my *idioma*, and that was exactly how Pamina liked it. Many times when the three of us were together, she pretended he wasn't there, initiating conversation only with me in my native tongue.

At first I usually responded in Spanish as a feeble attempt to include Victor, but Pamina was more persistent than I was. We ended up babbling away in

English while Victor pretended not to care. Although he had an excellent poker face, his ears were clearly tuned to what we were saying. He scanned every foreign syllable that escaped our lips for some trace of possible meaning.

Certain words: Yes. No. Day. Month. Pregnant. What. Serious. True. Father. When.

El hombre y el oso

"I feel for kissing you right now."

Is what Pamina shouted in my ear that night in *El hombre y el oso*, the gay club she had spent the last month nagging Victor to take us to. She complained that he was not taking her sexual frustration seriously, that he just rolled his eyes.

She told me she was *hastiada de los hombres*.

She told me heterosexual lovemaking was an act of spite, an act of violence.

She told me she was eighteen.

She told me she had never orgasmed but was sure she could if a girl sucked her pussy.

She told me she liked the word pussy, and also the word butterfly.

"What?"

I hoped I had misheard her. We were standing directly in front of the speakers, drowning numbly in the waves of sound and light.

There was a feeling of urgency.

Her hands were around the back of my neck, fingers laced into my hair, hanging on me like a necklace so heavy I couldn't stand up straight. She stood on tiptoe.

We were both angry at Victor at the time but for different reasons. When we were getting ready to leave, he had burned my thigh with his cigarette, leaving a dime-sized hole in the black tights I borrowed from my roommate. In Pamina's case, it was the twenty euro Victor had asked to borrow from her earlier that day and the six hundred euro he had yet to return to me.

He was waiting for us outside. (*No soy ningun maricón!*) I suspected that Pamina's advances had nothing to do with her attraction to me; she was merely attempting to punish Victor, to demonstrate her power, to threaten him, to send him a message.

I am back in your life and all of your possessions now belong to me.

Los perros de Sevilla

The dogs in Seville are all the same size. There are no purebreds. There are no strays. There are no leashes because there is no leash law. No leash law is necessary because the dogs are well-behaved. The dogs are well-behaved because they have to be.

A week before Pamina moved out of Victor's apartment, she looked up from her gazpacho and announced she was getting a dog.

"I need something to care about." was her only explanation.

I went downtown with her the next day to the house of the "dog woman," as Pamina called her. While we walked, Pamina told me things I did not want to believe about Victor and his half-sister. By the time we arrived, I felt the bitterness in my cheeks which means there are tears ready.

The dog woman was spectacular and enormous. She lived in a loft above a hookah bar and wore a vest made of human hair. Walking into her home was like being punched in the nose by a fist made of tobacco, peaches, and dog shit. She kissed us on our foreheads as we entered and asked if we were sisters. Pamina said yes, so I spent the remainder of our visit speaking as little as possible, knowing I would not be able to imitate Pamina's accent. Spanish dipped in Swedish.

The two puppies were playful with one another, nipping and tumbling, but they were also completely silent, which unnerved me. I sat on the floor and the white one crawled into my lap. I stroked his fur. Pamina liked the black one.

Eres un osito! she cooed at him. *Un verdadero oso!*

("You are a little bear; a veritable bear.")

The dog woman asked Pamina various questions, and Pamina told her all of the appropriate lies. A permanent residence in the countryside, a big yard, no job but plenty of money. And most importantly, a talent for knowing exactly what people most and least want to hear.

Un problema, said the dog woman, I cannot let the black one go alone. They need one another. They are a pair and cannot be separated.

"The white, it was scrawny. It would not have thrived," Pamina assured me on the way home.

Los inmigrantes

Victor was born in Medellín, Colombia, the most violent and beautiful city in the world. He suffered from a mysterious affliction of the kidneys which caused his cheeks and ankles to swell with waste. Whenever he took a piss, the whole neighborhood recognized the odor.

At twelve, he started smoking.

At fifteen, he lost his virginity to his history teacher.

At seventeen, after his grandfather died, he moved with his older sister to the south of Spain and was instantly cured of his childhood disease.

His grandmother had gone for a walk (*o algo*, Victor told me, a bit vague on the details), and he and his grandfather had just had an argument; I don't know what it was about, even though I once came very close to asking. The last thing Victor said to his grandfather was, *Te odio. Nunca volveré a esta casa.* "I hate you. I will never return to this house." He came back an hour later to discover his grandfather hanging from the rafters by a necktie.

He enrolled as a student of economics and accounting at La Universidad de Sevilla, knowing full well he would never graduate. He wasn't interested in a degree and was entirely unable to manage money.

Even when he owed me hundreds of euro, he insisted on buying my drinks, especially when Mario and Fernando were around.

He prided himself on his independence, supporting himself by working at the business his sister owned. It was a *locutorio*, an international call center for immigrants living in Spain to contact their families back home for a reasonable price. It had four cubicles, each with a stool and a phone. Victor sat behind the counter five hours per day, watching the customers come and go, seeing their dramas play out through the windows in the cubicles.

When there was nothing interesting to overhear, no sobs, no shouts, he checked his Facebook or watched instant replays of soccer games online. His favorite team was Barcelona.

La pesadilla

Pamina told me that she and Victor had been siblings in exactly seven past lives, which explained their current relationship: they could not stand each other, but they could not live without each other.

"Although we have been lovers last year, we were

not supposed to do; he is my spiritual brother." Her English was decent, and her Spanish was even better, but she did not talk like a local in any language.

In one life, she explained, she and Victor had been the son and daughter of a rich merchant.

In another life, two sisters in a peasant family.

In another, two brothers, one killed young at sea.

In another, twins who died in the womb.

In another, orphans.

In another, conjoined.

And once, Victor was a murderer.

Pamina learned of her and Victor's fraternal past from some psychic, apparently, some Norwegian psychic who, according to Pamina, would analyze me by phone for a mere one hundred fifty euro.

"I swear, you must to call her. She will make everything clear. I can tell you are one who requires spiritual guidance. An hour's conversation with her, and you will not cry for Victor anymore. She can help you."

One morning Pamina shook me awake in a tearful panic, having dreamed of Victor drowning.

Juliet

Victor's half-sister had tried many times to persuade her mother to quit smoking. She begged, made threats, stole and destroyed countless packs of cigarettes.

One day, when she thought her mother was at the grocery store, she lit a cigarette and dropped it into a pile of burning newspapers in the center of the kitchen. Even if it meant burning the house down, she had to send her mother a message. The house did burn down, with her mother still inside.

Juliet and Victor shared a father, but he was never spoken of.

Juliet was twelve years older than Victor and disturbingly beautiful. I sometimes caught myself staring at her, lost between the perfect angles of her face. I am told that when she arrived in Spain, she began working as a prostitute in order to support herself and her younger brother. One of her clients, a multi-millionaire, fell in love with her and became her husband. Now, Juliet owned her own business, lived in a mansion, and drove an enormous black Hummer with a minifridge and two television screens.

She pulled up one day in front of Victor's apartment

and invited both of us to come over for a swim. Summer had begun, and the air was forty-five degrees Celsius. At first I was ashamed to be seen in a swimsuit since my belly had grown so much, but spending the day with Juliet and her daughters, swimming, eating pizza, stroking the ears of their arthritic dog, became one of my fondest memories of my time in Seville.

Mugre

Tú y yo somos como uña y mugre.

Victor said it to me once. "You and I are like a fingernail and its filth."

I briefly wondered which I was supposed to be, the fingernail or the filth, until Pamina informed me, very matter-of-factly, that I was weak, that Victor had me firmly under his thumb.

La primera vez

We had to leave the bar early because Pamina walked out in a rage. I don't remember why. Victor pursued her, and I pursued him. He caught up with her in the street and put his arm around her, kissed her neck and stroked her hair and calmed her and loved her. I walked ten paces behind, bleeding salt and makeup out of my eyes. I considered leaving them then, turning silently down any side street and returning to my host family's apartment, but Victor and Pamina would not have noticed I was gone. They would have returned to Victor's room and slept together without guilt.

So I followed obediently behind, trying not to see, trying not to think.

By the time we arrived, Pamina and Victor adored each other once more and had vowed never to fight again and were closer and stronger than ever. I sat down on the couch, crossed my legs, and stared straight ahead. They embraced for a long time. Still partially in Victor's arms, Pamina bent over and kissed me on the top of the head before going upstairs to sleep in Victor's room. Without saying anything, he turned off the light and came to the couch, sat on top of me, straddled me, and commenced the familiar overtures of fucking.

"Victor … "

I said. I told him. I spoke his language. I explained in a language he could understand.

No soy una persona que suele decir que no este feliz …

"… but I am not happy. Obviously, that which

you have with Pamina is something very, very special. To say it is even more difficult because Pamina delights me and I believe that she is a very good people. But the truth is that it hurts me to be with you both together. I feel as if you two were the pair, and I the extra person. I will never ask you to choose among me and Pamina, but I now say that I cannot continue as your girlfriend."

The air in the room became thick. Victor melted off the couch and put his head in my lap. He cried wetly into the folds of my skirt, begged … *Quédate conmigo cariño. No puedo vivir sin ti.*

So I apologized and gave him head and soothed him until he fell asleep.

La corrida de toros

Victor, Pamina, and I went to a bullfight. There were six bulls and three bullfighters, all under the age of twenty. Even though I had extensively researched the stages of a bullfight and the origins of its various traditions, nothing could have prepared me for that first bull. I felt sick to my stomach and couldn't stop swallowing.

The second bull got his horn stuck under the

protective armor of the bullfighter's horse. Both animals died, still attached to one another.

The third bull became disoriented and rammed directly into a wall, shaking the entire stadium. His horn broke off, and he staggered around squealing and vomiting until he was declared unfit to fight and was shot.

The fourth bull trampled and gored one of the banderilleros.

The fifth bull refused to die.

By the time the final bull was being slaughtered, I had been somewhat desensitized to the violence.

Pamina smoked a cigarette and drowsily muttered about the barbaric Spanish culture. Victor cheered at the appropriate times, never taking his eyes off the magnificent spectacle.

Paco

When I first arrived in Seville, the Andalusian accent was difficult for me to parse. It gradually became easier, except when my señor was talking to me. Even on our last day together, I had to ask him to repeat himself more slowly when he bid me goodbye. His airy, toothless slang was unlike any Spanish I had studied in high school.

His name was Paco, and he was a heavy smoker. His cough was incredibly violent, the sound of lungs turning themselves inside out. Sometimes after a coughing fit, his words would drip with blood. His snore was a sucking, gasping struggle.

I told Victor that Paco was so bald you could read his thoughts on his forehead. "Don't laugh!" *Algun día tendremos un hijo así!*

Due to his health problems, Paco rarely left the apartment. He always slept through his alarm, which didn't matter since he had nowhere to go and no appointments to keep. At mealtimes, he ate and talked and listened to the radio at the same time, while also working on a crossword puzzle and watching sports on television and swearing heavily when his team was losing. I learned many new words from him.

Carmen

Carmen and Paco, my host parents, had been married for thirty-eight years when I met them, and they had dated for nine years before that. Paco was much older than Carmen.

In some ways, Carmen had become the head of the

household. Now that her husband was retired, she was the primary breadwinner, providing for her family by cooking and cleaning and laundering for international students like me and Cha-Cha. She led the conversation at meal times and sat in an armchair at the head of the table.

Pero a la vez, Carmen was a housewife, quickly silenced when she talked over the television. Paco was the only one to speak of politics or finances, and his decisions were always unquestioned. Carmen described him, always under her breath and to no one in particular, as *muy machista*.

They bickered about the appropriate volume of the television and whether or not to open the window in the dining room. Their squabbles always had a rhythm and a cadence, a tension and release, a kind of art, a kind of poetry.

El chocolate

Pamina did not view her bulimia as a disease, but rather as a lifestyle choice. We discussed it as we sat next to one another on a park bench and watched Victor and the Moroccans play soccer.

Pamina snacked on the bar of dark chocolate she

kept with her at all times wrapped neatly in gold foil. She broke off pieces of the chocolate in little triangles. Some pieces she held in her mouth until they melted, making her speech syrupy and bitter. Other pieces she swallowed whole as if they were pills.

"You will never be able to leave him you know." Pamina said, suddenly noticing the way my gaze was locked on Victor. "I think you have a taste for sex now."

Mario y Fernando

Victor once told me that he did not have any friends, only brothers.

When the Moroccans evicted him from his previous apartment, Victor found Mario and Fernando. By chance, Fernando and Victor owned the exact same jacket, and when they both wore it on the same night, they knew they would get lucky.

Mario was the only Spanish one. He once asked me, in consolation: *Por qué lloras por él? Es solamente un colombiano. No vale para nada aquí en España.*

"Why do you cry for him? He is only a Colombian. He is worth nothing here in Spain."

There was an expression only Mario's face was

capable of making, and I only saw it when Fernando was around.

Apodos

Everyone must have a nickname in Spain.

Among his friends, Victor was *el colombiano* ("the Colombian") or sometimes *el padre* ("the father"). What I preferred to call him was *el ganador* ("the winner"). To the victor go the spoils. He loved that.

I accidentally called him Hitler once, by mistake, not to his face. I had just been reading about Salvador Dali's painting "The Enigma of Hitler" and asked Mario when Hitler would be home.

Mario was *la mariposa* ("the butterfly"), *el maricón* ("the fag"), or María ("Maria").

Fernando was from Mexico, so I came up with el *golfo de México*, since *golfo* is a Spanish word meaning both "gulf" and "delinquent."

The three of them together, Victor, Mario, and Fernando, were Los Warros, which I never really understood.

Many times, the Spaniards accidentally called me Pamina, although I'm not sure I would consider it a nickname per se. I guess I was still *la otra rubia*, since Pamina was, in my mind at least, "The Panama Canal," that which separates North America from South.

La habitación

Pamina was moving out. She had been living rent-free in Victor's room ever since her arrival, but, due to a dispute with the landlord over an eighty-euro utility bill, she had decided to find a new living arrangement.

She would not return to Sweden, not yet. She was going to spend a few weeks living with Amine and Elias, two of Victor's Moroccans, both of whom were desperately in love with her. She told Victor that she had already found her own place, knowing of the bad blood between Victor and Amine.

She walked first, leading the way, I a step back from her, and Victor lagging almost a block behind. He was wondering what we were saying, what we were laughing about. His walk was slow and effortful as he struggled to manage the unwieldy cardboard box containing shoes, hand weights, and a dehumidifier. I was clumsy with the suitcases, one in each hand, full of clothing, makeup, and cigarettes. And Pamina's burden consisted only of a potted plant, the magnificent purple orchid she had purchased from a blind man in Portugal. It was a half-kilometer-or-so-long procession from Victor's place to La Plaza de Armas where Victor hailed a taxi to bring Pamina to her new home. After sealing Pamina neatly into the cab and sending her in the direction of La Alameda, I expected to feel lightness, ease, a burden lifted. But the walk home was treacherous.

El personaje is what Victor sometimes called Pamina. It means "the character." Alternatively, *el personaje con pies*, "the character with feet."

La llamada

One afternoon, when I was lying in bed staring at my cell phone and trying to make it ring, I overheard my *señora* in the next room. She was on the phone with one of our neighbors, a shriveled woman who wore a different wig every time I saw her. My *señora* must not have realized I was there.

Te digo de verdad, nunca he visto una chica con tan poca sal en la cabeza!

"I'm telling you, never have I seen a girl with so little salt in the head!"

El baño (1)

I had been crying in the bathroom for about twenty minutes when Pamina found me. She locked us into a stall and sat me down on the toilet seat. There was no toilet paper, and neither of us had brought tissues, which was problematic because my face was flowing down the front of my shirt in a stream of tears, makeup, mucous, and saliva.

I was getting over a cold, and I had just seen something I did not want to see.

"What the bastard!" Pamina muttered under her breath as she peeled off one of her socks and used it to dry my face. She touched her palms to my cheeks and spoke sweetly, softly. She kissed me on the left temple and on the back of my right hand.

Tomorrow, she promised, she would feed me strawberries and milk and I would feel refreshed, like a new person. "You must be only you and say fuck to the rest!"

Her words were strangely comforting to me. I thanked her many times and apologized for ruining her time with Ali, one of the Moroccan guys she had been sleeping with.

I decided to take a taxi home.

Veronica

Veronica was the adopted daughter of my *señora*, Carmen. When Carmen's mother was dying, the family hired a girl from Ecuador to help care for her. Veronica was fourteen at the time and had just been disowned by her family for getting pregnant.

Carmen's mother suffered a protracted illness. She had to be lifted from her bed to her wheelchair several times per day, a repeated task which left Veronica with a hernia and a twisted spine. By the time Carmen's mother died, Carmen had grown to love Veronica as an adopted daughter.

Veronica had warned me about Latino men, always out of earshot of her fatherless daughter, Bea, who was now eight.

La cara de poker

Victor once explained to me: *para ser buen jugador de poker, es necesario no saber que eres buen jugador de poker.*

It means "in order to be a good poker player, it is necessary not to know you are a good poker player."

We were lying in his bed, and he whispered into

my hair "I … like … yousomoshhhh." It caught me completely off-guard. He was a different person in English. His voice was higher-pitched, whiny, childish. He sounded exposed and vulnerable. And it would have been uncharacteristic of the low, breathy, Spanish-speaking Victor to offer such a gem, unsolicited.

And *te quiero*.

And *te amo*.

Mágico

I know three card tricks. The first is very easy to execute as long as you understand the concept behind it. The second involves sleight of hand, which requires a bit more practice. The third is actually magic.

In the third trick, the face cards become characters in a story which I tell as I lay out the cards. I ask my audience-member to cut the deck and shuffle it repeatedly, but the cards always come up in the correct order.

I showed Victor my tricks with his poker deck in order of impressiveness. At the first two tricks, he was amused and delighted, but when I performed the third trick, he was outraged.

"How the fuck did you do that?"

He made me repeat the trick many times, closely scrutinizing my every move, requesting that I roll up my sleeves or stand on the other side of the room. The trick worked perfectly every time, as I knew it would, and he was furious. He demanded to know how I had rearranged the cards and accused me of keeping secrets from him. He became hysterical, swept the cards to the floor, held me down on the table.

La cicatriz

When I arrived in Spain, the soft, white underbelly of my left arm was still perfect. Smooth, hairless, immaculate, intimate. A baby's skin. The skin that only reveals itself in moments of puzzlement or surrender or ecstasy.

One strange thing about Victor was that he owned an iron and an ironing board. His clothes were never dirty or clean. He showered twice a day and immediately after sex. His bathrobe was mildewed. Mounds of laundry cluttered his room. To dress himself, he fished an article of clothing out of some pile, sniffed it, and, if it passed inspection, ironed it. He always looked good.

I tried to teach him the word "dapper" because I knew it would be useless to him.

Me pareces un chico bastante dapper, I said.

Victor had never forgotten to turn off the iron before, but the first night I lived with him, the iron was left on. Silent and sinister, insidious on his floor. It stood on its back, reared up with the metal plate facing me, a cobra poised to strike.

Victor was in the shower. I was dressing, or undressing, I don't remember which. I noticed a pink piece of paper on the floor, a post-it in the shape of a heart, with ink in an unfamiliar handwriting. I bent over and reached towards it, accidentally brushing against the tip of the iron.

Burns do not bleed. They do not reveal their severity right away but fester and swell and undergo many transformations. But the scar is permanent, a tiny triangle, branded onto my body in the unmistakable shape of a V.

El baño (2)

My feet were perpetually filthy, which bothered Victor. He himself hated walking barefoot and hated it even more when I did.

One day, we were watching television in his living

room, an incredibly stupid show called *Tonterías las justas*, when he suddenly scooped me up in his arms like nothing and carried me upstairs, leaving the television on. He was not angry. He took me to the bathroom and sat me down on the toilet seat, kneeled down, and delicately placed my feet in the bidet to wash them. He patted them dry and set them gingerly into his extra pair of slippers.

Sabes, he said, *la única cosa más grande que mi amor para ti es mi miedo de perderte*. "You know, the only thing greater than my love for you is my fear of losing you."

La última vez

Pamina was gone, and Victor's landlord was not happy. Victor had started to avoid the landlord, dodging questions about Pamina's whereabouts and the unpaid utility bill. The landlord became fed up and evicted everyone. We had two weeks.

The night we received the eviction notice was one of the hottest nights in the city's history. I lay with Victor in his bed, trying to make as little contact as possible with his sleeping, sweating body. His irregular snoring had sometimes kept me awake in the past, but that night was unbearable.

I already knew what would happen: Victor would move in with his half-sister temporarily and then take the vacation to Sweden he had been talking about. The semester was over and my host family already had new guests. Even if I could have returned to them, my pride would have made it impossible.

The next day when Victor was at work, I moved my two small suitcases into a hostel across town. I met Pamina for coffee two days later at *el café de siempre* to tell her I was leaving. She was sunburned, having spent the previous day at the beach with Victor.

The Girl with the Egg-Shaped Face

by
Mohita Nagpal

New Delhi, 7 a.m., January 25

The aisle popped up with heads as the string of my till-now loyal rucksack came off upon stepping into the bus. The bag went face down with a thud, looking like an obese man spread out on the floor. I turned a little red at having lost my anonymity even before the journey began.

"Get your bag out of the way, you are blocking the passage," barked the conductor.

I picked the bag and headed towards seat number thirteen. A largish English woman was already seated there, next to a woozy man I assumed to be her husband. To avoid any confrontation, I didn't disrupt the harmony of the couple's life and moved towards the two vacant seats near the rear door. I sat with an involuntary sigh, a note of thanks from my aching back.

The bus seemed new, with the shiny metal surfaces bearing a proud, expectant feeling. I glanced around. On my right, two stocky marriageable techies were staring forlornly out the window. Behind me, a glum mother was dissuading her over-enthusiastic son from trying to work out the mechanics of a suspicious looking TV screen, and a girl was fruitlessly trying to convince her father that she would be able to complete the journey without being molested or leched at.

Diagonally to my right, two girls were giggling to themselves. The seats directly in front of me were occupied by two bosom-heavy girls, who were co-participants in the little giggle orgy. From their careless laughter, they seemed to be college girls. From their apparent disregard for male company, they seemed to be from a girl's college. And from their topic of discussion, they seemed to be heading exactly where I was going.

Literature festivals have become to English students what pilgrimages are to people of my father's generation. An annual deed to be executed with thousands of other believers. As I chewed on this sociological phenomenon, the engine screamed out in pain, the driver touched the photo of Lord Hanuman sitting on the front windshield and swore at someone at the same time. The journey began.

The two girls sitting diagonally from me blushed and shrieked in excitement and superficially clutched each other the way happy people do to usher in journeys. The one sitting on the left had already taken off her red sneakers and now sat crossed-legged. She tied up her curls, put on her nerd glasses, bent towards the girl sitting in front of me and, in a whisper, cursed in her ear, "*Bhenchod*, I forgot to pee." Her friend laughed with unrestrained mirth while I managed a restrained smile. She sensed my smile and turned back to catch me just as I was hurriedly returning to my somber composure. She smiled and said something to her friend and the two giggled in half-embarrassment, half-disregard for what the world thought of them.

I gazed out of the window at the yawning trees, the expectant roads and the thinning houses. I began to watch her again, this time taking note of the shade of her eyes, the faint lines of existential crisis on her forehead, the curious shape of her face. Almost egg-like. Positively egg-like. I have kissed a face like that before, I thought.

In a gloomy hotel room in Agra, I had kissed

The Girl with the Egg-Shaped Face

an egg-shaped face that summer. Tia was four weeks pregnant with her boyfriend's child and had just given herself an abortion. She was wailing in agony and I had kissed her tenderly on the forehead to soothe her pain, unsure if it would be morally okay to take any pleasure in that kiss and afraid her boyfriend might suspect the love I was trying to suppress.

But the girl in the bus had a broader forehead. What would it be like to kiss her forehead, I wondered. She took out a beefy paperback. An attempt at justifying her trip to the Jaipur Literature Fest, I thought.

I tried to sleep but, instead, pictured the sequence where I entered the bus and tried to gauge the egg-faced girl's reaction. She didn't seem to have noticed me despite the noise my bag had made. I pressed my eyelids harder in the hope that it might alter the reality. I again pictured the scene, this time letting fantasy take its course and saw her looking at me curiously.

She was holding the book in her left hand and fighting her uncooperative curls with her right when I opened my eyes. I squinted to catch the title of the book. *Atlas Shrugged*. I wondered if it would be justified on my part to make any judgments when I myself was unsuspectingly carrying *Anna Karenina*. I took out the new purchase and began reading.

Mohita Nagpal

The bus had stopped for a fifteen-minute break when I woke up. I had drifted off to sleep while reading. I noticed the bus had not stopped at the place designated for government buses to halt, but at some expensive-looking resort. I thought of voicing this concern when the egg-faced girl broke into a noisy yawn and asked no one in particular why the bus had stopped there. I wanted to say that I had been wondering the same thing. But my voice never left my throat, as if caught up in the middle of a powerful current.

At the food court, I greedily tucked into a sandwich and went out carrying powdery coffee in a paper cup. I had just dialed an acquaintance in Jaipur who was supposed to find me a cheap place to stay there when I saw the four friends tracing their steps back to the bus. The two bosom-heavy girls in fact looked not so bosom-heavy while walking. They were just two jovial plump girls wearing similar-looking clothes and expressions. The third one had a troubled, constipated look about her and looked like the sort who grows nauseous during bus journeys. And my girl (and that's when I realized I had started thinking of her as my girl) was gazing absentmindedly ahead. Walking unconsciously, she was moving from sheer momentum, looking like a picture of dreamlike innocence. She entered the bus and I kept gazing at the spot where she had been standing for a moment longer than I had intended.

The engine revved up, this time releasing just a shrill cry. My girl had swapped seats with her nauseous friend and was now seated near the window. I could no longer see her without achingly tilting my neck and making obvious to the other passengers what I dared not confess to myself.

I pulled a borrowed iPod from my bag and began untangling the earphones. The conductor did a round of the bus to issue tickets to the new passengers. I idly asked him how far Jaipur was.

"Two hours," he said, disinterestedly.

I nodded and resumed my struggle with the headphones.

"Excuse me," a mellow voice said to me.

I looked up. It was the girl with the egg-shaped face, tilting her delicate neck to negotiate a generous view of me. My face grew hot and I started feeling a strange sensation in my stomach that I had not experienced since my senior secondary exams.

"Yes?" I replied, trying to sound unruffled.

"What did he say? How long will it take to reach Jaipur?" she asked.

So she heard me. Has she been noticing me all

along? Has she been looking for a reason to strike up a conversation with me? I blushed at the thought.

"Two hours," I said, with such affected indifference that I was shocked at my own cold manner.

"But it usually takes much more than that," I immediately added with a smile, in an attempt to make up for my rudeness.

She nodded and disappeared from my view. I quietly reproached myself and thought up more questions for the conductor.

The iPod was playing the Beatles when she stretched, got up and stood in the aisle to talk to her friends. I took off my headphones and focused all my faculties on her. They were discussing a group of college girls they were expected to meet in Jaipur. Her face grew wickedly excited as she discussed the bitchiness quotient of the group's ringleader.

I stared at her more boldly now. She sensed my glance and looked at me. Our eyes met. Mine embarrassed and diffident, her questioning and curious. I was the first to look away, afraid of revealing anything more than I intended to. After a moment, I watched her again. She had made a seamless transition to the gossip session. But there was something different now. Her eyes had a knowing look, accompanied by something that could be read as both anger and acceptance.

I put back my headphones. Paul McCartney was crooning "And I Love Her." I wondered if the ballad was trying to say something to me and immediately brushed away the thought. Love on the road is fragile and short-lived. And what were the chances of her being interested in a girl, I reasoned with myself.

I didn't look in her direction again, pleased at having successfully averted probably the seventh heartbreak in the twenty-five years of my life.

February 2

I paid for my overpriced cappuccino and checked out of the cafe. I took the escalator to enter Rajiv Chowk Metro station in Delhi. I was supposed to meet Sanya at 1 p.m. It was 1:45 p.m. already. Sanya is my best friend, my confession box, my conscience-keeper, my spiritual mother, and she is always late.

She met me with a warm smile and an equally warm hug in an attempt to make up for being late. I let myself be easily manipulated. We were headed to a former colleague's place in Karol Bagh where I had self-invited us for lunch.

She had bought a teddy bear for Aradhya, our host.

"You don't buy a 35-year-old a teddy bear," I said.

"Age can't diminish a woman's love for teddy bears," she said, trying to sound wise.

I smiled with a condescending shake of the head and stepped into the tube with her.

Her phone rang. It was Aradhya. "Hi, so sorry we got a little late... ," Sanya started explaining.

I glanced around. A woman was coating her nails with paint the color of ear wax, a man sitting next to her was self-consciously picking his nose, and an old man with the demeanor of a retired insurance agent was side-glancing lecherously at a woman. An extended family from a village was spread out on the floor near the gate, unsuspectingly blocking the way for people to enter or exit.

"I told you not to trust him with your secrets. He's an asshole," a girl screamed to someone on a phone. My head turned, along with all the others in the coach, to look at her. The girl looked around embarrassedly before continuing her conversation, this time in a hush. I turned back to face Sanya. Sensing something familiar, I turned again. Next to the girl on the phone stood a girl reading a paperback. My heart froze. I turned to Sanya, who was still on the phone. I turned again. It was her. Positively her. The girl with the egg-shaped face. A coincidence. A beautiful coincidence.

Sanya had put down the phone. Sensing something strange on my face, she asked me what was the matter.

"That girl standing behind me with a book in her hand was on my bus while I was going to Jaipur," I said.

We both looked at her. "Don't you want to say hi to her or something?" Sanya asked.

Yes, of course. Why hadn't that struck me in the first place? I wondered.

"Hi," I said to her.

Startled, she looked at me confusedly.

"I was on your bus while you were going to Jaipur. I was sitting behind you — "

I stopped when she cut in with a smile of recognition.

"Oh yes, I remember. You were reading *Anna Karenina*," she said.

"And you were reading *Atlas Shrugged*," I said, pleased with her reply.

We looked at each other for a few seconds like that, cherishing that moment of serendipity.

The taped voice announced the next station. We were supposed to get off there.

"So, where do you live?" she asked, breaking the spell.

"Lajpat Nagar, we were just going to a friend's place in Karol Bagh," I said, pointing towards Sanya who had moved towards the gate.

"You are from Delhi University, right? I remember overhearing your conversation," I added cheekily.

She nodded with a smile that bordered on a pleasant laugh.

The train reached the station. "Sorry, I have to get down here," I said, and pushed off, thrilled by the short encounter.

On our way back from lunch, Sanya and I stopped for coffee. In one of those intervals of meditative silence, I smiled to myself.

She asked me what was the matter.

"It's that girl," I said. "That meeting," I paused. "What a coincidence."

"What are the chances of you meeting someone like that? I mean we could have boarded the Metro a minute earlier or a minute late or entered some other coach and I wouldn't have met her. But that didn't happen. You were late and we entered the very coach she was in. That's something. Do you know what I mean?" I said.

She contemplated what I'd said.

"Nothing is a coincidence. Everything has a design," she finally said. "You should have asked her name. You could have looked up her on Facebook and become friends."

And then, like a lightning, it struck me that I didn't know her name. Everything had happened so fast that it hadn't occurred to me to ask her name. I had made some stupid small talk, but forgotten to ask her name. I mentally rebuked myself, more and more harshly.

"But if you are meant to be friends, maybe you will run into each other again," Sanya said, sensing my agitation.

Her words pacified me a little. Of course we will meet again, I thought. We are meant to meet again. Otherwise, why would I have run into her today? What would have been the purpose of that? We will meet again. Just like today. Out of the blue, when I am not expecting it.

February 3

I woke up tired. I had many dreams last night. The kinds that are so vague you are unsure where one ends and another begins. Though I didn't remember them, I felt there was something pleasant about them. I closed my eyes, trying to remember.

I had been thinking about that girl before I slept. Maybe I dreamt about her. Maybe I met her again, I thought. Maybe I asked her for coffee and we went to a little cafe where we shared our life stories.

She told me she'd wanted to speak to me on the bus but hadn't had the chance. She'd felt there was some chemistry between us the very instant she'd seen me and thought we had an impending kiss between us.

I pampered my imagination with these fertile seeds of love.

She had asked me where I lived. Why would she ask that? Could she be also thinking about me right now? That meeting in Metro ended too soon, with too many things left unsaid.

I lay on the bed, staring at the ceiling in the hope of finding some answers.

We are destined to meet again. Till then, I have no other option but to live in this slippery world of hope, a voice told me.

No, I can't just sit and wait. I have to do something, a second voice addressed me, jolting me out of my reverie.

I made a plan. I thought of visiting the places

where I might run into her. I tried to guess how she might like to spend her evenings. All I knew about her was that she was from Delhi University, a student of English and probably from a girl's college.

If she had taken the pains to visit the literature festival, she might also be attending book events in Delhi, I thought.

I opened the newspaper to check upcoming literature events. But I didn't even have to start reading before it struck me that a book fair was to begin the next day.

Yes, a book fair. Nothing could be more timely. This seems like god's will. Happiness seized me and I lay down on the bed in ecstasy.

February 4

I didn't meet her. It rained in the morning, washing away the event as well as my hopes. Not allowing myself to be discouraged, I pledged to try again the next day.

February 5

I bought seven books I had no intention of buying, helped a German professor pick out some South Asian literature, and bought a second-hand Gabriel Garcia Márquez with a crumpled love letter inside that revealed it had been gifted to someone on the exact same date seven years earlier. I prophesied that these were signs of something bigger to come. But I didn't find her.

I came back home and lay lifeless on the bed. It was never going to be easy. How could I have been so naive? I wondered. It's over now. I have lost my only chance. The little love taking shape in my heart will never grow up to become a flower.

I have irrevocably lost her.

February 6

I woke up with a plan that had come to me as an inspiration either in a dream or some deep meditation.

With my heart on tiptoe, I went to the bus stand from which I had boarded the bus for Jaipur. I cooked up a tale of how a girl on my bus had borrowed a novel of mine and I'd forgotten to take it back. Now, after ten days, I had realized that it contained some very important documents of mine. I also dropped in the fact that I was a journalist.

The bored-looking "uncle" behind the counter

gave me a kindly smile, good-humoredly reproached me for my stupidity and began to browse through the bus charts in a nondescript file.

But my search hit a deadlock sooner than I had anticipated.

The office had records only for the month of February. I would have to go to the main bus terminal some twenty kilometers away, file a written application to the officer-in-charge and then wait for the bureaucratic process to unfold at its own unhurried pace before hoping to lay my hands on the chart.

"Uncle, please find some way. It's urgent," I said, all puppy-eyed.

He offered me a cup of tea and dialed someone to find out if there was an easier way out of my misery. And there was one.

He switched on a computer of a kind I thought had disappeared from the surface of earth two decades ago and clicked on a file that contained all the bus routes for 2013.

I fed him the details. A chart appeared on the screen. Blood started rushing to my head. I sensed he could hear its movement. I grabbed the printout. It had the first names and ages of all the passengers.

Four names stood out to me from the rest.

Shilpi, Anisha, Shreya and Shivani. All aged twenty-one. One of them was her. Her identity was now narrowed down to just four names in the universe.

At home that night, I switched on my laptop and took out a sheet of paper. On the left side, I made a list of all the girls' colleges in DU. On the right, I wrote the names of the four girls.

I opened Facebook, a sophisticated improvement on the Yellow Pages for the love-sick. One by one, I carefully typed each girl's name along with each of the colleges in the hope of running into her profile. It wasn't ever going to be easy. But it was tougher than I had anticipated.

I got up after five unrewarding hours. I was done with seventy percent of my search combinations. I was spent — physically, mentally and emotionally. With my eyes red, mind numb and heart bleeding, I went off to sleep.

February 7

I woke up early despite having gone to sleep late. I switched on the laptop and resumed the search. I had gotten over the previous night's gloomy mood, yet I had a hunch that I would probably never see her again. But I kept on searching, trying to dig through the earth with a thin-bladed knife.

Four hours later, I called it quits.

I pretended not to be disappointed and told myself that it was a silly crush all along, that I was letting myself get carried away by stupid romantic ideas. I was just in love with a coincidence, I affirmed. I blamed the unintelligent Bollywood movies I grew up on for my irrational behavior. I'd noticed her on the bus just because her egg-shaped face reminded me of Tia and my lost love for her, I told myself.

And then, imagining her face I grew weak again. I began to visualize us together in an open field, now on an empty street, now at my home.

I show her my room. She admires my guitar and asks if I play. I tell her I am a terrible musician. She asks me teasingly what I am good at. I tell her I am tempted to say something really cheesy. "What?" she asks, coming closer to me. She stops just a few inches from me. We are very close. We can feel each other's breath. I look her in the eyes. She doesn't look away. We stay like that for the longest time. I put my arms around her. She smiles through her eyes. I kiss her softly, first on her eyelids, then on her lips.

I woke up feverish. I had fallen off to sleep. More like, I had made myself sleep in order to stop myself from drowning further in my fantasies.

I was in turmoil. All my tranquility and petty pretensions had fallen away. I switched on the laptop and thought of starting the search process again. But I didn't. Instead, I arbitrarily typed the four names together on Google. The first few results threw up attendance reports from some commerce colleges. Towards the latter half of the page, I saw the fourth-semester English results of Miranda House, a girl's college.

Feeling the flow of life again in my body, I clicked the link with gentle fingers, afraid any force might alter what was going to come up on the screen.

The four names were now complete: Shilpi Wadhera, Anisha Lal, Shreya Sabharwal and Shivani Jha.

I typed the first name on Facebook and stopped breathing.

My eyes welled up with tears of joy. I felt bliss fill up my body.

She was called Shilpi Wadhera, what an unfitting name I thought. I had long addressed her as the egg-faced girl in my head and her real identity kind of unsettled me.

She was smiling down at me from the computer screen in an almond-green sari, unaware of the euphoria unfolding within me. She liked *Pulp Fiction* and *Death Proof.* Jane Eyre and Dante. Simon and Garfunkel and Neil Young. She had a Dalmatian and a room with purple walls. She loved bagels and black coffee. She was a feminist, agnostic, film buff and, most importantly, thought herself capable of falling in platonic love with women.

❧

So this was the design Sanya was talking about the other day. That's why she resembled Tia, that's why I was attracted to her, that's why I ran into her in the Metro, and that's why I had the inexplicable urge to meet her again. I sighed. But how do I approach her now? Sending her a friend request might alarm her since I am not supposed to know her name. It would be just perfect if we met accidentally, I thought.

I checked her updates. She was in Chennai for a wedding, with her friends Shreya and Shivani, the bosom-heavy ones from the bus. Her friends had posted some pictures taken outside the hotel. In the background, I could faintly make out the name, Hotel Fox Tree.

I pulled my rucksack from the closet and began to pack.

February 8

The perspiration in the air greeted me the moment I got off the plane. Even with the sun smiling cynically and the auto drivers quoting obnoxious rates, I felt strangely in control.

On reaching Hotel Fox Tree, I went to the front desk, made an extra effort to be polite, offhandedly dropped in the fact that I had lived in Chennai for a year, and collected my room keys.

Then, stopping as if suddenly remembering something, I casually enquired if someone by the name of Shilpi Wadhera was staying in the hotel.

The manager checked his computer. A frown and an impending no appeared on his forehead. What about Shreya Sabharwal? I asked.

This time, he answered in affirmative. "Yes Ma'am, she is staying in room 101," he said.

I thanked him and proceeded to my room, feeling cheerful.

After a quick shower, I went to the patio area in the hope of some early luck.

I ordered a coffee and began reading a paper. Two girls took a couch next to mine. I looked up and it took me a while to realize it was the bosom-heavy duo. My girl was not to be seen. I pretended to read the paper.

I began wondering where she was. Was she in her room? Was she going to join these two girls?

"Excuse me," one of the girls said to me.

"Yes," I said, trying to appear calm.

"I might be mistaken, but I think you were on our bus from Delhi to Jaipur last month," she said, speaking for the other girl as well.

"Oh, yes. Of course, I remember," I said, looking surprised.

"In fact, I ran into a friend of yours the other day. That girl with curly hair and glasses," I added.

"Shilpi? She is also here with us," she added.

"Oh, how wonderful," I said, releasing a relieved sigh.

"Where is she by the way?" I said after a pause, trying to make it sound like an afterthought.

"She must be on her way — "

"Here she is," said the other girl, pointing to her right.

There she was. In flesh and blood, her hair still a shiny wet from the shower, eyes unable to conceal their grogginess, a knee-length turquoise dress adorning her slender body.

She noticed me from afar. Our eyes met and instantly communicated. It was unlike the first two meetings.

"Oh my god! I can't believe this. What a coincidence," she said, her words sounding superficial compared to what her eyes were conveying.

"This is unbelievable," I said in similar tone, looking right into her eyes. I could see my reflection in them and knew she was looking at the same in mine. At that very moment, something passed between us, something very subtle and inexplicable. It was as if some unknown force within us had taken over while we stood tight-lipped, preferring that mode of communication.

And then, in an instant, everything was revealed without having been said. She knew. A faint smile of acceptance played on her lips.

"So what brings you here?" her friend asked me, thinking the silence uncomfortable.

"Some unavoidable office work," I replied to her while looking at Shilpi.

She smiled at the word unavoidable, as if telling me she knew what I meant by that.

"How did you like the Jaipur festival?" her friend asked me.

"I think I came back a different person from that trip," I replied, and looked straight ahead at Shilpi, laying bare everything I was holding back.

Her expression underwent a subtle change, as if slowly acknowledging the real meaning of my statement.

"You guys are here on a holiday?" I asked her friend, in order to make things a little less obvious.

"We came for a friend's wedding. But it has been a very boring trip for us," she said.

I looked at Shilpi. "Not for me," her calm serene eyes seemed to be saying to me.

"Oh, it's already 11 a.m. We are late. We have to catch a bus for Pondicherry," her friend said, looking at her watch.

"Pondicherry," I repeated, and looked at Shilpi. Suddenly, her face lost its glow. Her soul seemed to have retreated into her shell. Something had snapped. Our reality had altered.

"Yes, Pondicherry. We are going to meet Shilpi's guy there," her friend said.

I looked at her with wounded eyes but she refused to meet my glance and looked away.

"Would you like to come along?" her friend asked me.

I searched for an answer in her eyes and found one.

"No, I have work," I said with an apologetic smile, drawing strength from some untapped reserve.

"Then we will catch you in the evening," her friend said, and turned away.

The other bosom-heavy one also shifted the weight of her legs in order to move.

I looked at Shilpi, conscious that faint drops of tears had begun to take shape in my eyes. She looked at me, her face losing its color.

We stood like that for a few seconds.

"Goodbye then," she said. The sound had a strange, heavy edge. She seemed to have held back her words and rolled them multiple times on her tongue before saying something entirely opposite.

"Bye," I said.

Her friend called out to her. She turned and began walking. That was our final farewell. I knew it and so did she.

She turned once to look at me. She seemed about to say something, but didn't. She turned again and didn't look back.

The Girl with the Egg-Shaped Face

Our Unlikely Fusion

by

Danusha Goska

In the summer of 1987, I gazed across the noisy, crowded lobby of the Piast student dormitory in Krakow, Poland. My eyes hit upon a man against the far wall. He looked typically Polish. He was the figure I'd select for a union striker on a Solidarity poster. I decided to walk across the lobby and start up a romance with this man. Our romance would be my entrée, as a tourist, into the Polish soul.

He was a bit shorter than I, and a bit older. His clothes were decent and conservative but not the newest, nor the most stylish. His pale cheeks were stubbled; his hairline was receding. I would devote a page of my diary, later that summer, to an attempt to describe his eyes, his, to me, at that moment, typically Polish eyes. What I would tell my diary was that his eyes had witnessed great sorrow, but that they still knew how to laugh. By the time I had crossed the lobby, I had my irresistible pick-up line carefully scripted.

"Excuse me, do you have the time?" I asked, in Polish.

"I'm sorry," he replied, in English. "I don't speak Polish."

Darn!

From Canada, he now lived in Rochester, New York. His name was Laurence Skopitz, and he was a rabbi.

That is the last time I remember not being friends with Rabbi Laurence Skopitz. In every other memory, we are pouring out our souls — often late into the night — we are arguing — sometimes quite heatedly — we are not letting the bastards grind us down, we are trying to understand God and to practice "*tikkun olam*" — the repair of the world — we are singing, and we are laughing.

❧

I went to Poland in 1987 to re-expose myself to Polish stuff. Born in New Jersey of immigrant parents, I'd been living in Africa, Asia, and the People's Republic of Berkeley. I hungered to eat dill soup. I craved to walk through fields of rye and poppies, and to hear the *hejnal*, the historic trumpet tune played every hour from the steeple of a gothic cathedral. I yearned to be annoyed in the way that only a Pole can annoy me.

That summer that I returned to Poland, the Jagiellonian University was hosting a groundbreaking conference on Polish-Jewish relations. I was not part of that group. I did not even know what "Polish-Jewish relations" was. Rabbi Laurie was a participant. Laurie told me that he and other Jews had traveled to Poland because, "We don't want any guilty parties to get off without consequences." Any and all Poles were potentially among the guilty. Including me.

In September, 1939, World War II began in Poland. The overwhelming military machine, Nazi Germany, invaded from the west. Hitler declared, "I put ready my Death's Head units with the order to kill without pity or mercy all men, women, and children of the Polish race or language." The Soviet Union invaded Poland from the east, and began, methodically, to erase eastern Poland. During six years of war, millions of people, including my own family members, were enslaved, exiled and massacred. Many Jews allege that Polish Catholics did not do enough to stop the Holocaust. Many Polish Catholics feel that Jews do not honor Polish suffering and heroism.

I remember an old woman from Laurie's group. She spoke of watching Jozef Pilsudski, war hero and statesman, march into Vilna, her city, to reclaim it as Polish. She had rushed out, along with all of her neighbors, to greet him and his troops with patriotic joy. She spoke with intense yearning of the apple tree she had seen outside her window as a child. After the war, anti-Semitic campaigns drove her into exile. She never stopped missing her apple tree. She wanted it back, every leaf, flower and fruit, even if only in spirit, even if only in the way she told her stories, this Jewish woman wanted to lay claim to her childhood home, to her very own Polish apple tree.

How did Rabbi Laurie and I contribute to the ongoing dialogue between Polish Catholics and Polish Jews? This is what I remember: I remember that Laurie's roommate, Rabbi Paul Saiger, had brought with him to Poland a suitcase whose entire contents was granola. Was he afraid of the notorious food lines in Communist countries? Or of being trapped into eating non-kosher food? Or did he just really like granola? I didn't ask. I thought Laurie looked Polish; he insisted that I looked Jewish. I couldn't be, I told him; I like ham. I remember one night we were out at a club, and a Byronic figure from Laurie's group kept persistently flirting with me. This man was a child of a concentration camp survivor. He used his sadness to lure people in; once he got them close, he used his steroidal rage to punish them. Laurie didn't like this guy one bit. "You do not need a narcissist." Even as this melodramatic figure kept luring me with his dark eyes, tragic tales, and need, Laurie would put his hand lightly on my knee and extemporize yet another spontaneous comedy routine. Laurie kept me in stitches, bent double laughing, so that I would not break free from his protective orbit, and spend the night with the moody bad boy.

Laurie teased me about my feet. He took a photograph of my feet. He said that I had the biggest feet he'd ever seen. "Epic. Monumental."

He said to me, "You travel a lot. Who misses you when you leave? You are a person who should be missed."

I remember feeling really sad when the Polish-Jewish group departed, and I was left with the Polish-Gentile tour group. The conversations I craved to finish had all departed with the Polish-Jewish group.

I remember Laurie insisting to me, with real fervor, "You can change Jewish people's minds about Polish Catholics. You changed my mind."

How? I don't remember a single pertinent political, theological, historiographical thing I said to the Polish-Jewish group. I remember the granola, the laughter, and Laurie's eyes.

People ask if we were lovers. We couldn't be. Rabbi Skopitz worked actively against the marriage of Jews to non-Jews. I was outraged, offended. "How can you obsess on this?" I taunted him. "While the world faces environmental catastrophe. Look at global warming!"

"Jewish survival is much more important than global warming," he said.

I rolled my eyes. I realized there was nothing for us to say to each other. So we moved on to the next conversational topic.

Laurie told me about a woman he found attractive. One day she cried because it began to snow. He acknowledged that her reaction was extreme, but he couldn't help but be aroused — she was so delicate, so feminine, so needy. My big feet and strong-like-bull bohunk constitution could not compete.

❧

That summer spent in Poland changed my life. I

decided I needed to write about Polish-Jewish relations, a field I hadn't even known existed before I took the trip. There was so much pain. There was so much love — indeed, some referred to relations between Poles and Jews as a "marriage." There was so much opportunity for healing. If we could figure out, people like Laurie and me, how to heal the wounds of Polish Catholics and Polish Jews, we could figure out how to heal the world. This healing, I was sure, would begin with words. I vowed: my words would contribute. Whatever magic had happened between Laurie and me in Krakow would extend to my readers.

When I was a kid, I would read biographies of writers, and I would come across this phrase: such and such a king or fan or spouse "supported" a writer. I never read that sentence about non-writers. No one ever talked about "supporting" lumberjacks or roofers. I wondered if writers were like three-legged stools that required propping up.

I get it now. After twenty-five years of writing about Polish-Jewish relations, I get it. When I recognize one of my students as particularly gifted, I pull him aside. I don't do that to tell him about the barrel of laughs that's in his future. Writers must see new things, or old things in a new way. We must say what others are not saying. That job description of writers also meshes with the definitions of "insane" and "political prisoner."

Writers wonder about themselves: Maybe you really are delusional. Maybe propriety is correct. Maybe a decent person would keep her mouth shut. What if speaking renders you unemployable? Will the poverty, the slum address, the lack of health care be an apt trade for these mere words? Why not just sit back and wait for someone else?

Rabbi Laurence Skopitz supported me. No money changed hands. After the weeks we spent together in Poland in 1987, we never saw each other again.

Laurie returned to Rochester, New York. My big feet returned to the road: Berkeley, Poland, Turkey, the Midwest, New Jersey. Graduate school and a PhD. Our relationship — emails, phone calls, letters — was like John Donne's "fix'd foot."

When I first started saying things, in print, about Polish-Jewish relations, I tried to do a writer's job, and the job of a healer. I tried to see things in a new way, and to propose new routes to wholeness. Academics backed away from me slowly as if I might explode. Caring others warned me that I'd never get a job, publication, or funding. I was denounced by both sides. Publishers eagerly solicited my book, told me it was unique and necessary, presented signed contracts, and then apologized profusely. "Too controversial." Academics must publish or perish. I was perishing. Winters without heat. Food banks. Charity care. Year after year, crushing disappointment after crushing disappointment, Laurie kept saying to me, over and over, with the persistence of April raindrops: ignore the naysayers, ignore the naysayers, ignore the naysayers … keep talking, keep talking, keep talking … it will all be worth it someday, it will all be worth it someday, it will all be worth it someday.

Rabbi Laurie supported me in a way I didn't know people could support each other. He supported me more than I knew how to support myself. Laurie believed in God. Tapping God's infinite love and faith, Laurie never needed to worry about running out. He expressed his love and faith through the language of his tradition. I don't know if we ever talked without his telling at least one tale from the Talmud, or singing a traditional Ashkenazi folksong. The weave between the ancient past and the modern man was seamless.

Sometimes synchronicity seemed to boldface our

connection, through all our differences, and the miles between us. One late night in Berkeley, Laurie and I were chatting long distance. I was whining about a Buddhist I had fallen in love with in Nepal. Laurie insisted that I had to hear a traditional Jewish folksong, that it would explain everything. He began to play his clarinet through the telephone.

My radio was making strange sounds. I interrupted Laurie. I listened to the KPFA deejay, who said he was playing "*Shofar*-Tibetan bell fusion." *Shofar*: the traditional Jewish ram's horn. Tibetan bells: what I heard on the wind when I loved the Buddhist in Nepal. Wildly different puzzle pieces coming together to shape a suddenly harmonious whole.

I quizzed Laurie about synchronicity. In the book *Rescuers*, I read of Stefania Podgorska, a Polish Catholic teenager from a simple background. She didn't even know her own birthday. She had no resources. Her loved ones had been taken to Germany for slave labor. She was suddenly mother to her six-year-old sister. During the Nazi occupation of Poland, Stefania saved the lives of thirteen Jews. When the Nazis were closing in, Stefania heard, and obeyed, a disembodied voice that gave her explicit instructions on how to shelter her Jewish charges.

Our Unlikely Fusion

It's a heartwarming story, but we must demand: why didn't God speak so clearly to millions more?

Rabbi Laurie answered, "Maybe God did try to communicate with others. Maybe they didn't listen."

❧

In 2006, Laurie told me that he was ill.

I decided, "I can't handle this, I'm not going to think about it, and he'll get better." I can't even tell you the name of the illness. I continued going to Laurie with my woes, and expecting him to comfort me. He did.

I was planning to speak at a Polish-Jewish event. I was feeling some burnout. For once, I wasn't sure what I'd say.

Rabbi Laurie sent me this email: "Well, you could say: 'I have some trepidation about speaking at this forum tonight, possibly because of stereotypes that get in the way. A lot of people ask why I didn't save any Jews, even though I was born many years after the war. Before coming here this evening, I shared my concerns with my dear friend and mentor, Rabbi Laurence Skopitz of Rochester, New York, who reassured me. He reminded me that I have something very important to say, and that, perhaps, like water penetrating the stone at the well in the story of Rabbi Akiba, my message will make sense to those who are willing to listen with an open heart, who appreciate contradiction, nuance, and who recognize that in life there is very rarely black and white, but only shades of gray. I hope to encourage you to consider new ways of looking at old problems and re-stimulate a dialogue, which has been ongoing between Jews and Poles for almost a thousand years.' Anyways — feel free to say that you're my pal and that I think you're brilliant. I will send you an amulet for *parnasah. B'matzliach*."

☙

On November 16, 2006, Laurie wrote, "The last time I was on a roller-coaster, I instinctively kept my eyes closed painfully tight, and screamed in abject terror throughout the whole three-minute ordeal. For me, coping with illness, all the delays in treatment, hopes, assurances, disappointments and detours, have been very much a roller-coaster ride. However, with this ride, despite all the ups and downs, I have managed to keep my eyes open and, for the most part, resisted the urge to scream. A phone call yesterday seems to have changed all that. Things are moving uphill again and appear back on track."

A couple of weeks later he wrote to say that he was feeling better. "I had to be at the hospital by 7:30 a.m. I have never understood 7:30 a.m. A professor once told me that 'a true philosopher never rises before noon.' I have always aspired to be a true philosopher. 7:30 a.m. is what can be called an ungodly hour. God didn't invent it: we did! If God wanted us to be up that early, he would have created us with built-in alarm clocks."

A couple of weeks after that, it wasn't Rabbi Laurie who wrote, but Temple Beth David. The subject line: "Update on Rabbi. Your Prayers are Needed. Importance: High." The email included the words: "Please do not call and do not visit."

Later that day another email went out. Subject: "Come to a *minyan* tonight." A *minyan*: the ten adult Jewish males necessary for public worship. This was a prayer service called for Laurie. There was a distant Polish Catholic woman present that night — in spirit.

The morning of Saturday, December 16, I went to the adjunct office on campus to do some work. I switched on the computer in a crowded, noisy room. I looked at the screen and said, out loud, "No."

"It is with great sadness that I have been asked to report to all of you that Rabbi Skopitz passed away last night. He was with his family and passed without pain. All was done in accordance with his expressed wishes and in accordance with Jewish law. A rabbi was present."

❧

The rabbi who was present was Michael Herzbrun, an agnostic. After Laurie passed away, I asked him, "Give me a message, Laurie, that I can share with your friend and colleague Rabbi Michael, that will prove to him that you are still with us, and that there is life after death, in order that Michael might regain his faith in God."

I sat quietly for a moment. A word popped into my head: "Azure."

"Azure? Laurie, you've gotta be kidding me."

I sat quietly for another moment, awaiting a more appropriate omen. "Azure."

"C'mon, Laurie, really. 'Azure' is not the first color one might think of in relation to Poland or Judaism ... "

But the images just became more insistent: the color itself flashed across my mind. Azure water. Blue sky. The word, written out.

"Okay! Azure it is."

I emailed Rabbi Herzbrun. I asked him what the word "azure" might mean to him and Laurie.

Nuthin.

☙

Time passed. My book on Polish-Jewish relations continued its rocky path from publisher — "Innovative! Probing! New! We have high hopes!" — to suddenly frightened publisher — "Too controversial. Sorry." The list of potential publishers was exhausted. It was certain that the book would never find publication. It was all the harder given that Rabbi Laurie was no longer there to believe in me, to urge me on, or to make me laugh, in late night phone calls to Rochester, New York.

And suddenly, out of nowhere, a publisher appeared. Suddenly, the struggle, its unheated apartments and long days of research and writing on no income, was in the past.

On February 16, 2010, I finished the final editing and sent the manuscript off. Immediately after that, I was walking to campus along a tree-lined road frequented by turkeys, deer, and red-tailed hawks. It was a dark day in a dark winter. I have to wonder if statistics don't reflect that New Jersey's shrouded winter of 2010 contributed to, if not an increase in the suicide rate, at least a mass outbreak of Russian-novel-reading along the New Jersey Turnpike.

Snow was falling thick and fast. Life in a snow globe: I lost my tenuous hold on a sense of "up" and "down," "here" and "there," "then" and "now." There's something anti-gravity about a thick snowfall. A dark form approached: my student. He was hatless; snow sprinkled his fluffy hair. His arms were outstretched, as if to catch snowflakes on his dark sleeves, to check if there really are no two alike.

I was obsessed. After a lengthy wilderness pilgrimage, I'd sealed the publishing deal. But that wasn't my students' focus, and I needed to be a teacher, to turn my focus from my own work to my students. I tried not to think about the book or the momentousness of the day, or the fact that I didn't have anyone near-at-hand with whom to celebrate.

This approaching student, this image emerging from the shape-obliterating snow, had deeply challenged and vexed me.

One recent day during office hours he had stopped

Our Unlikely Fusion

discussing his final paper and began to talk about his childhood in Bosnia. He told me that one day after work his dad had returned to his suburban home with its many windows. He wanted a smoke. He walked to the kitchen table to get his cigarettes and a neighbor with an automatic weapon began to spray the house with gunfire. His dad hid under the stairs for the next several hours. Later, he ran. When running, he favored cemeteries. He believed that the Serbs were too superstitious to pursue him there.

Once, when my Bosnian student was a kid, a child near him dropped an ice cream cone on a city sidewalk. My student squatted down and began to eat the other child's ice cream cone. His mother began to cry, but she didn't stop him. Her son was hungry.

That childhood memory, the ice cream cone incident, occurred in July 1995, when eight thousand Muslim men and boys were massacred by Serbs in Srebrenica.

My student mentioned Brcko, his hometown, to me. I turned from him, to the office computer, and did a Google image search of Brcko. I expected to see photos of picturesque villages and mountains. Instead, there were photographs of crushed and bloodied corpses, some stretched out and arranged in rows on morgue slabs, some crumpled, random.

There was a photo of two men on a sunny street. The men have their backs to the camera. The closest man is wearing a blue shirt and grey pants. The man in front of him is wearing a red sweater and blue jeans. The man closest is holding an automatic weapon up to the head of the man in the red sweater; that man is cringing, as if to protect himself from heavy rain or a falling branch. In a subsequent photo, both men are lying on the ground; streams of dried blood clot about their heads.

My student showed no reaction to this photo. He said to me, casually, "You know, I would never indicate the number three by holding up these fingers," and he pointed to the fingers he meant. "Because the Serbs, when they were massacring us, used to hold up those three fingers, to indicate 'Father, son, and Holy Ghost' and, after they massacred us, they would chop off our fingers. My goal is to become a forensic anthropologist, so I can return to my country, and identify corpses. One of my family members was just identified after sixteen years."

One of the rewards of old age is being able to share

Our Unlikely Fusion

lessons with the young. "You don't know how to do that? Here. I'll show you. Voila! Problem solved!"

In writing my book on Polish-Jewish relations, I had focused on the past. I met men who, their heads suspended between hunched shoulders, books stuffed under their arms, appeared never to enter the twenty-first century, to be always lurking outside its doors, aggressive with their assertion that they had the inside scoop on exactly what went down in 1648.

There was a humanitarian justification for this obsession with the past: "Never again." We had to understand the Holocaust, so it would never happen again. We had to read the next book, the next thousand books, attend the next debate between the usual combatants. Each pugilist might merely repeat exactly what he had stated in his previous debate performance, but he might place the semi-colon in a new spot; we had to be present for that.

I know this sounds incredibly stupid and naïve. We haven't fixed things. We are passing on to young people a world where "never again" is empty syllables. Feeling utterly impotent and dreading the future young people face: not one of the rewards of old age.

As my Bosnian student spoke, lines from W. H.

Auden's poem, "The Shield of Achilles," went through my head:

> A ragged urchin, aimless and alone,
> loitered about that vacancy; a bird
> flew up to safety from his well-aimed stone:
> that girls are raped, that two boys knife a third,
> were axioms to him, who'd never heard
> of any world where promises were kept,
> or one could weep because another wept.

In the poem, Auden alludes to the crucifixion of Jesus. I ask students why Auden does this. "This is an allusion. It is anachronistic." I turn to write "allusion" and "anachronism" on the blackboard. "Why would Auden place Jesus in a poem about the Trojan War, over a thousand years before Jesus was born?"

Maybe I'm asking the question wrong, but my students never give the answer I suspect is true: Auden is saying that the time on the clock or the calendar page does not matter. "Never again" is a catchy slogan; that's it.

As my Bosnian student spoke, I craved the release of tears. I did not feel I could cry in front of my student.

I wished I could go home and phone Rabbi Laurie and re-purpose our plan for world salvation, for *tikkun olam*. But Rabbi Laurie was gone.

ℰℛ

Even our classroom was dark that snowy February day; it was a basement room, windowless.

Once a semester, I require my students to present folklore. They can do anything they like, from African drumming to hula dancing.

On this day, a group of students dramatized the legend of the Golem of Prague. I quietly began to weep. My very first scholarly publication on Polish-Jewish relations addressed Prague's Golem legend. And now, in 2010, all these years and all this struggle later, as I shipped my book off to the publisher, my students, who didn't know about that article or the book, out of all the folklore they could have chosen, chose to dramatize the Golem.

The synchronicity felt especially poignant to me because the journey to publication had been so long that many people I wished could share this moment with me — my immigrant parents, Rabbi Laurie — were dead.

I looked at my students. They'd blush if they knew how adorable they are to me. Dressed as Jews in Prague: there were paper beards and Salvation Army fedora hats. They were piecing together body language and accents from films and visits to New York City, trying to act like Eastern European Jews. It was especially poignant because the student playing the rabbi was my Bosnian student, who was, of course, a Muslim.

And suddenly, it became even harder, in this low-ceilinged basement room, to hide my tears. Because I suddenly realized that the first name of this student, this student who was acting out the very legend that began my journey of publishing on Polish-Jewish relations, this Muslim rabbi for whom I wanted so badly to repair the world, through my work, through my teaching, through something — that his first name was that very unlikely word, "Azur."

All That You Forgot to See

by

Naima Lynch

"To burn with desire and keep quiet about it is the greatest punishment we can bring on ourselves."

— Federico Garcia Lorca

Althea often felt as though she didn't see things properly, as if others were always pointing out things she ought to have noticed; the fullness of the moon or the cuteness of a baby, the shades of a sunset or details in the architecture that she passed through every day. "Spring is in the air," a coworker might say to her, walking in ten minutes late, cheeks flushed, wearing linen pants and a flowing blouse, "I just had to walk the long way to work!" Althea would nod and make an oval with her mouth, feeling suddenly confined in her drab winter sweater, wondering why she hadn't noticed the change.

What Althea did notice, what she could become positively fixated on was the detritus, the collateral damage of humanity. She could spend long minutes tracing the outline of a stain on the carpet with her eyes, wondering at its shape, guessing at its origin. Coffee? Motor oil? She was easily distracted by the transformations of food; anxious about the way we are always ingesting and subtracting, putting things in our mouths until they disappear; distraught over the way a slice of carrot cake arrived in a tidy triangle on a clean white plate, only to be eroded and reduced like a sand bar; so many orange crumbs and smears of frosting. She marveled at the violence of forks and knives.

So entranced had she been one morning on the N train, watching the elaborate choreography of a homeless man's morning ritual, that she'd missed her stop. She'd stared obliquely as he undressed down to his loose, gray underwear, draped his clothes across the eggshell blue MTA seats, and peed into a water bottle, unperturbed by the huddle of passengers holding their noses on the other side of the carriage. She'd marveled at the way he'd tended to his feet, carefully wrapping them in strips of fabric, swaddling them in newspaper, before lowering them into his decaying shoes. She'd

All That You Forgot to See

never given one thought to how or where a homeless person might perform these ministrations of survival, and though she was vaguely worried that he'd suddenly turn on her or perhaps even hurl his bottle of urine, she was impressed by his skills.

Still, it's not as if Althea could have breezed in twenty minutes late to Trowell, Byer & Clingman, announcing to her coworkers that she'd missed her stop because she'd been hypnotized by a homeless man; "spring is in the air!" is by far a more acceptable excuse. Chances are her coworkers wouldn't have noticed her absence, anyway; they'd be chatting about characters from shows she didn't watch, telling stories about kids she didn't have, rolling their eyes about husbands who, in Althea's imagination, were all variations of Mr. Brady and Ricky Ricardo; these caricatures of masculinity, oblivious to the inner machinations of their household, were all that came to mind at the word "husband."

❧

Where her habit of missing the bigger picture became most problematic was during the annual summer holidays she took with Globetrotter Travel &

Tours. For the last twelve summers, she'd taken two weeks off in August to join the guided tours offered in the glossy Globetrotter catalogue. The first time she'd been invited, prodded really, by Lorraine, both of them having turned fifty-three that year. Lorraine had decreed that they'd officially earned the right to travel in packs, be herded onto buses and ferries, coerced into wearing matching hats and forgoing the pressure of selecting hotels and arranging meals. "I always secretly wanted to travel this way," Lorraine confided over iced-tea on the balcony their two apartments shared, and then proceeded to regale Althea with tales of mosquito-ridden camping trips, the indignities of hostels, and the various parasites and diseases she'd contracted all in the name of youthful adventure. "Bring on the laminated itineraries!" They'd clinked their glasses together in agreement.

They'd gone to Ireland. Joining the rest of the tour group at Dublin International Airport, they'd blended in just fine; two women in their fifties, neither with a wedding ring, in matching orthopedic walking shoes and sun visors. They sat next to each other on buses, their wide bottoms spreading across the seats, laughing at all of the driver's bad jokes, lifting their double-chins

All That You Forgot to See

towards the places he announced on his microphone — "and to your left you can see the bathroom window on the third floor of Van Morrison's old house." Althea always at the window, while Lorraine preferred the aisle — an arrangement Althea found absurd seeing as how Lorraine was always leaning across her to point at things in the landscape that Althea could never quite make out.

Back on their balcony in Queens, listening to an Enya CD, they'd sat putting pictures from their trip into the identical shamrock-themed photo albums they'd purchased in the airport. Althea didn't take many pictures; when the bus stopped for compulsory photo-taking, she'd just pointed her camera in the direction everyone else was aiming and hoped for the best. Lorraine had a real camera, with different lenses and special settings, and she was always going on about shutter speeds and f-stops. Lorraine had bonded over cameras with a man in their group, Jim, a retired dentist traveling with his wife Joan. Jim and Joan were fit and sprightly, and engaged in copious amounts of public affection while buying rounds of Irish whiskey for the whole group. Once, while Lorraine and Jim had been comparing cameras, Joan leaned over jovially to Althea and said, winking, "I could care less for f-stops, as long as they can find our g-spots!" Althea had immediately started sweating, and tried to pretend as if she hadn't gotten the joke.

Is that what people think, Althea wondered, that we're a couple?

It's true, neither of them had ever been married, nor did they have much experience with men; any experience in Althea's case. The only time the topic of her perennial virginity came up was with her gynecologist, who'd scribbled a note or checked a box and that was the end of that. While Althea and Lorraine discussed most everything, their conversations never veered towards past love affairs or escorts to dances. Might as well discuss the last time they'd visited the moon or speared a fish, so unrelated was the topic to their lives. Althea and Lorraine had inhabited apartments 1A and 1B, respectively, for fifteen years, and had managed to avoid ever discussing their avoidance of all things sexual. It wasn't hard to do; they were both of an age and physicality that effectively excluded them from being viewed as such; no longer subjects or objects, of or with, desire — a status Althea found relieving.

When she was younger, people would ask Althea

All That You Forgot to See

about her marital status, whether she'd procreated and such. She'd find herself stammering such soap opera phrases as, "Oh, Mr. Right just hasn't come along yet," or, "I'm sure he'll come when I finally stop looking." But it'd been many homogenizing years and many obfuscating pounds since anyone had thought to ask her. Joan's blithe between-us-gals comment had blindsided her; where had she gotten the idea? Sure, Althea and Lorraine sometimes held hands while they watched *60 Minutes*, but that was all, and it didn't mean a thing. Althea avoided Joan for the rest of the trip.

Lorraine had printed doubles of all her photos, separating them into two stacks, one for each of them. "Oh look!" Lorraine would say, her drugstore glasses perched on the tip of her nose. "Remember that?" Lorraine handed Althea photos of the Giant's Causeway shot from interesting angles, of Celtic tombstones pinstriped in light and shadow, of the perfect reflections of boats in Galway harbor, not a ripple in the water, with names like *Gusty Gracie*, *Insubordination*, and *Midlife Crisis*. Althea was dumbfounded by the photos, especially the ones which featured her own perplexed face, candid shots of her profile taking in the thundering sea or resting on a bench in front of the Belfast murals.

Her mouth always open in a perpetual yawn. She didn't really remember the moments. It had only been a week since they'd returned and already she had to concentrate hard to conjure the places they'd been. Goodness, had she really been standing that close to the edge of that cliff? Had she really stood in the gates of that enormous castle? Where had her mind been?

Althea had found Lorraine dead on her spot on the couch, a bowl of tortilla chips in her lap, a puzzled smile on her face as if she'd died playing *Jeopardy*. The coroner said it'd been a stroke, as sudden as turning off a switch. When Althea packed up all of Lorraine's things, she'd come across a cache of old Polaroid photo albums under her single bed. In them, Althea saw a younger, slimmer Lorraine with bouncing blonde curls and tanned shoulders. Many of the pictures showed Lorraine with another woman, tall and willowy with long black hair. In one of them, they're sitting on a porch swing with their long legs draped over each other, making peace signs, handwritten in the white strip below, simply: 1977. In another, Lorraine looks happily surprised to have been lifted off the ground from behind, two girlish arms tight around her waist: Italy. And there was one where Lorraine had turned the camera around on their own two faces, off center and blurry, their rouged lips pressed together, freckles like seeds across their summery cheeks: Phyllis.

Sitting on the floor of Lorraine's bedroom, pictures in her lap like proof … evidence of … what exactly? The thought began to congeal in her mind for the first time, formless and vague, that she had loved Lorraine. She felt a surge of anger towards Lorraine, which quickly reshaped itself as jealousy towards this Phyllis woman, before finally settling as a knot in her stomach that closely resembled hunger. Skittishly, she superimposed herself into the snapshots. With her eyes closed and her hands folded neatly in her lap as if praying, she swung on the porch swing in a cloud of Lorraine's gardenia perfume, pressed her forehead between Lorraine's shoulder blades as she gripped her around the waist and lifted her like an offering; she saw herself applying the cherry-red lipstick to Lorraine's lips, beautifying and desecrating all at once, before smashing her own lips against them. Too precipitous, Althea knew; these thoughts, these indulgences, could unravel her. She added the box of photos to the trash pile.

❧

Althea wasn't sure why she signed up for the next trip, just a few months after Lorraine died. When the chirpy travel agent called her to see if she was interested, she'd just said yes. She supposed it was a kind of memorial for Lorraine, or an escape from the oppressive heat of New York City summers, but after the fifth or sixth trip, it had simply become habit. Besides, she'd officially become a Globetrotter Gold Member, enjoying special perks and discounts, which included an "I'm Hot to Trot!" t-shirt. She'd gone to France that second summer, trying her best to make friends and continuing to make half-hearted attempts at taking pictures. She returned to find Lorraine's apartment rented to a young college student who said his name was Duke, a name she found patently canine. He'd partitioned their balcony into two halves with a thin piece of wood, and Althea had to suffer his cigarette smoke and loud conversation while she placed her photos in the Champs Elysees album.

Her bookshelf now boasted eleven such albums, each one half-filled with the meager results of her disposable cameras. Washed out shots of Arctic icebergs, Big Ben with the top of its tower cut off, the sunburned backs of her fellow tourists waddling in for a snorkel in Aruba while she waited under an umbrella on the beach; photographic proof that she'd been in these places, even if all she could clearly recall was the hair she'd found in her soup or the missing blade in a ceiling fan.

Now, at sixty-five, Althea expected the call from Globetrotter any moment. "Hello there Ms. Dewall!" the voice would say. "Are you planning on another Globetrotting summer with us this year?" They'd proceed to tell her that this summer was going to be something really magnificent, that they'd been planning for months to make it the best tour ever. "The Bahamas!" they'd announce, breathlessly. "Australia! Croatia!" For a few weeks, she'd have something to say to her coworkers whose usual neglect had turned into overt disdain; they wanted her to retire, she knew, and had been trying to encourage it by ignoring her almost completely, as if they'd already retired the idea of her. She'd gotten slower at her job. When she'd started as a secretary at the law firm forty years ago, she'd basically been a glorified typist. Over the years her duties had expanded to include basic paralegal activities, and she'd managed to keep up. Lately, though, her bosses, who were not the same bosses as when she'd started, had begun to receive resumes from people who'd actually studied law, and whose grasp of procedures and technology far exceeded her own. "Well, I'm leaving for Mexico in two weeks," she'd blurt out awkwardly from within her cubicle, waiting to see if anyone responded, her thin voice dying in the air.

Ꮖ

When the phone finally did ring, Althea muted the television to take the call.

"Are you planning on another Globetrotting summer with us this year?"

"Yes."

"Great! We have planned a real adventure, Ms. Dewall, we are going to Egypt!"

Althea's mind scurried to drum up an image. She thought of pyramids, the Nile, ancient Pharaohs and scenes from *Exodus*. But that was all thousands of years ago; she was hard-pressed to think of any facts about modern Egypt without resorting to *Lawrence of Arabia*, and saw herself encircled by the imposing black-and-white specters of Peter O'Toole and Omar Sharif on horseback, their faces obscured by turbans.

When the information packet arrived in the mail from Globetrotter, she spread out the fact-sheets and what-to-pack tips in front of her. "In some parts of Egypt, women should wear headscarves out of respect," it informed her. "Some mosques will not allow non-Muslims inside, but many will." Althea felt a pit forming in her stomach. "The common response to *salam alaikum* is *walaikum salam*," the "Useful Phrases" pamphlet told her. Althea felt a chill course through her body. Headscarves? Mosques? Egypt, she realized, was full of Arabs and Muslims. What was Globetrotter thinking?

Althea was scared, and why shouldn't she be? She'd been in her apartment when the Muslims flew their planes into the twin towers, the chaos and fear pooling around her, swallowing the city whole. She'd made for the door to go check on Lorraine before remembering that Lorraine was dead; she had no one else to check on. Althea wasn't political, she didn't even vote, but she'd been alarmed by the possibility that Barack Obama might be a Muslim, the odd syllables of his full name keeping her up nights. She didn't go to church herself, but found that she was in agreement with those who said white, Christian America was under attack. There were Muslims all around her in New York City.

Sometimes she'd see one of the women who covered not just her hair, but her whole face, and she'd become enraged, not because she felt bad for the woman, but because she didn't think the woman ought to have the right to hide her face. After all, Althea couldn't hide her face. All around her neighborhood they had their special markets and butchers and food carts. She could hear them speaking their language, and see the confusing shapes of their letters on signs, and she always felt certain they were talking about her.

She wondered what Lorraine would do. Lorraine had been a high school English teacher and prided herself on being worldly and cultured. She'd loved the History Channel; Althea recalled watching a documentary on the Crusades, which had incensed Lorraine, who'd had no tolerance for arguments about God or religion. She'd been raised in a harsh Catholic family, and though she never discussed it, Althea felt certain that she bore the scars of an intolerant upbringing. "On both sides of this story," Lorraine had said during a commercial, "are regular people, wives and children and old folks, who are forced to be … you know, caught up in all this … zealotry, who have more in common with each other than the so-called religious warriors on the battlefield." Althea didn't know what she thought. For all her indignation, Lorraine was less judgmental than Althea, and always played the devil's advocate. She couldn't suffer hypocrites, and some of their only disagreements had been when Lorraine accused Althea of being one.

"Glass house," Lorraine would say when she thought someone was being hypocritical, and Althea would imagine their apartment building bursting into so many lethal shards. Watching a politician rail against abortion? "Glass house." Reading an article criticizing alternative parenting techniques? "Glass house." Another phrase she'd been fond of was "Get over it," which she applied more liberally, with a dismissive wave of her hand. At the end of the day, there wasn't that much that Lorraine had taken personally, and she blamed most of the world's problems on other people's pride. Althea imagined telling Lorraine that she was scared to go to Egypt, scared to be in an Arab country. "Get over it," Lorraine would tell her. But you weren't here when they did what they did! Althea would cry. "Glass house," Lorraine would say, calmly.

☙

There had been three other people on her flight who were also on the Globetrotter tour, a couple in their early seventies accompanied their fifty-something son. They spent the flight practicing their Arabic phrases, excitedly looking through the guidebook, while Althea wrung her hands and pretended to sleep. They landed at eight in the morning and rather than deplane through the air-conditioned tube connecting them like an artery to the airport, they were made to descend the stairs in the stifling heat, Althea struggling with her carry-on suitcase, and take a crowded bus to the terminal. They were greeted by Howard, the same guide who'd led them through Italy and British Columbia. He was holding up a big sign that read "Globetrotter" like a flame for gathering his moths. When they'd all assembled, Althea hoped she'd see a familiar face but none were present. Those that were there, the trio from the plane included, intimidated Althea. Although they were around her age, give or take a decade, they all seemed younger and stronger than she. Most of them wore shorts with lots of pockets and durable, sporty sandals. Althea eyed their tanned calves suspiciously. The women looked comfortable in loose, cotton tunics, just as the info-packet had advised, while Althea

All That You Forgot to See

sweated visibly in her gender-neutral button down shirt and "I ♥ New York" sweatshirt.

Salam alaikum! Howard said giddily. Walaikum salam, all his Globetrotter's replied while Althea moved her lips in pantomime. Howard went on to pass out laminated itineraries for the five days they'd spend in Cairo, and introduced their translator and local guide, Bilal. Althea hadn't even noticed Bilal standing next to Howard, so diminutive was his posture next to Howard's gregariousness. Howard and Bilal threaded them through the chaotic airport to the shuttle bus waiting to take them to their hotel. Bodies from all over the world jostled her, their odors assailing her, and she had a powerful urge to just sit down and cover her head with her arms. The others all carried big backpacks, as the info-packet had suggested, while Althea struggled with the same rolling suitcase she'd brought on every other trip, one wheel refusing to fall in line. When Bilal offered to help her, she was surprised by his New York accent. He saw her shock, and easily offered that his parents had both worked for the United Nations, and that he'd been raised in Brooklyn.

On the bus, Althea basked in the air-conditioning. Howard passed around their matching red hats and stood near the driver facing them. "We're heading to the world famous Shepheard's Hotel, depicted in Noel Barber's famous book *A Woman of Cairo*, which was on your suggested reading list." Most of the group nodded that they'd read it. Althea felt embarrassed, and hoped they wouldn't be asked to hand in book reports.

"The hotel has kindly arranged a late breakfast for us. At around 11:30 we'll take a nice walk over to the tower, the —" he snapped his fingers.

"Burj al-Qahira," Bilal finished.

"Yes," Howard continued, "and take in one of the best views of the city, which will help give you some perspective as we explore over the next five days. From there, we'll explore Zemalek, Cairo's own little island, where you'll see the famous Opera House, stroll down the beautiful streets where most of the embassies are, and do some shopping at the Yamama Center. Please exchange money at the hotel, as you'll be free to grab snacks and lunch at your leisure. We'll return to the hotel around six for a break, and then tonight we'll have a dinner cruise on the Nile with belly dancing!" He clasped his hands together excitedly and Althea felt nauseous.

Althea was exhausted, and increasingly felt that she'd made a horrible mistake. She pressed her face

All That You Forgot to See

against the cool glass window, trying to understand the landscape that was rolling out in front of her. The road leading them out of the airport was lined with hotels whose names she knew — Hilton, Marriot, Sheraton — names that soothed her. Many of the buildings they passed were large, concrete structures whose modernity took her by surprise. The asphalt roads themselves impressed her; she'd been expecting a desolate sandy expanse punctuated by palm-treed mirages. Bilal pointed out landmarks on their way to the hotel that Althea struggled, futilely, to locate before they'd sped past. At the hotel, their luggage was off-loaded by dark-skinned men in traditional clothing and cylindrical hats on their heads. The breakfast spread was full of fresh pastries and fruit and Althea realized how starving she was, piling her plate high with everything she recognized. She joined a group of her fellow trotters and did her best to be conversational. "Oh yes, so excited," she lied when they asked if she was looking forward to their grand Egyptian adventure. "A dream come true, for certain," her eyes wide with bewilderment.

Too much walking. So very hot. Why did everyone else seem so immediately acclimated while she felt so dizzy and disoriented? Althea had needed to stop and catch her breath numerous times along their route through Zemalek, and although no one openly chastised her, she could tell by the way Howard tapped his foot and checked his watch that she was holding up the group. By the time they returned to the hotel for their pre-dinner break she was utterly spent. She forced herself to shower, slathered her face with the same cold cream she'd used for forty years, and laid naked on the cold white sheets under the fan.

She was unused to this posture, supine and exposed, and it felt somehow profane.

She was more aware of her body in that moment than she could ever recall feeling. Her muscles were pulsing with fatigue, every pore on her body a little mouth gasping for breath. She could feel her shape, flattened across the mattress, its island-like contour. The hairs on her body oscillated under the fan's breeze. She was aware of her large breasts like two cats nestled into her armpits; her stomach a rolling landscape which prevented her from seeing her feet. Have I always lived in this body, she wondered, her eyes closed, have these

All That You Forgot to See

always been my legs? My arms? My face? Has this always been me? She thought of Lorraine's Polaroids, the dark-haired Phyllis, and suddenly felt a rush of longing that bordered on seasickness. Althea had no interest in longing, or in the clamoring of her own body.

Instead, she tried to recall all she'd seen on that first day in Cairo, matching the laminated itinerary of destinations and landmarks to the images her mind had managed to trap. She felt like both doctor and patient in an exercise to gauge dementia. Her memory played a silent film of the overcrowded airport, the buffet punctuated with items she couldn't identify, the comfortingly European hotel. She'd seen the Nile, Shepheard's was right across the street from it, but it had failed to register properly. Aside from the cruise ships and *feluccas* moored to its shores, its brown, muddy water, trash swirling in eddies, had seemed no more spectacular than the East River back home. She'd seen Egyptians, of course, and was surprised that so many of the women seemed so modern and stylish, many of them with their hair on display.

Still, the men scared her; the old ones with beards and robes seemed poised to sentence her to death, the young ones in blue jeans about to blow themselves up.

She was sure of it, and tried her best to keep her distance. Even Bilal, she thought, seemed sinister and secretive under all his helpfulness and familiar pronunciation, and she couldn't shake the feeling that he was planning to deliver them to some inescapable place. She was drifting to sleep when the call to prayer blasted through her windows: voices, crackling and staticky, blended together in a cacophony of preternatural sound, rising, falling, pausing, resuming in an alien cadence. She felt certain she would die in Egypt.

She'd skipped the dinner cruise and belly dancing, telling Howard that she was simply too tired and would just order room service, that she was sure she'd feel better tomorrow. He'd made no attempt to encourage her to join them. The next day's plans consisted of a morning visit to the Giza Pyramids, before the real heat of the day bore down, the Khan al-Khalili Market, Tahrir Square and the Al-Azhar Mosque. Dinner would be back at the hotel, where they'd be joined by a special guest: a poet friend of Bilal's who was going to give them a reading.

೮৩

She tried to see the pyramids through Lorraine's eyes, but her own eyes kept taking over. They were met by a group of men holding the reins of snorting horses, stamping their feet in the sand. Althea hadn't known it was to be a horseback tour, and her heart rate rose in alarm. While her compatriots were led away in saddles, she took in the view from the air-conditioned Pizza Hut conveniently located across from the grand structures, lethargically snapping photos through the window. From where she sat with her warm Diet Coke, she had a perfect view. The Sphinx crouched staring at her from across the road, smaller than she'd expected. Beyond it, she could plainly see the famous monoliths, three in total, rising out of the desert. She tried to feel something, to be awed; she knew that she should be. More than any other landmark or site that she'd been placed in front of on her summer tours, she knew this was by far the grandest, the oldest, and the most significant; yet, she couldn't help but feel underwhelmed, cheated somehow. Perhaps it was the Pizza Hut logo on the window, superimposed onto her view. It might've been the cars and fences and trash receptacles that prevented an unobstructed field of vision. Or maybe it was the universe of emptiness beyond them, the innumerable grains of sand, the impossible horizon and endless sky.

But she felt nothing, nothing except the empty void where wonder should've been, an organ gone missing, a phantom limb.

From the Pyramids, they were bused back to the heart of Cairo. They moved like a flock of birds in their matching red hats through the throngs in Tahrir Square, tread solemnly through the pillared courtyard of Al-Azhar Mosque before making their way to Khan al-Khalili. As they walked, Howard and Bilal informed them that Khan al-Khalili was one of the oldest bazaars in the world.

"It dates back to the fourteenth century," Howard told them.

"Watch out for pickpockets," Bilal added.

Entering the bazaar, Althea felt as if she'd wandered onto a movie set. In spite of herself, she was dazzled by the stalls boasting colorful scarves and sparkling jewelry, embroidered shoes with upturned toes that she caught herself imagining on her own swollen, arch-less feet. Corridors turned into rabbit holes; the choice of right or left felt momentous, almost heroic. This must be what it feels like to be an ant in a mud castle, she thought as they passed under the high, vaulted ceilings and made their way through the narrow streets, the thought brought a smile to her face.

She was so delightfully captivated that she forgot to feel harassed by the crowds of humans that pressed against her as they walked. Their destination had been a little café, Al-Fishawy, where Bilal told them Naguib Mahfouz, "the Hemingway of Egypt," had often come to write. They were served sugary coffees and pomegranate juice that came with a spoon, so thick it was with little juice-filled gems. Althea sparked a conversation with a couple in the group and learned that they were from California, had four grandchildren and were especially interested in Coptic churches. She was included in an impromptu group photo, and spontaneously wrapped her arms around the people at her side.

She found herself looking forward to dinner and the poetry reading as they made their way out the way they came. She was thinking about trying some new dishes, maybe practicing some of the Arabic phrases the others were tossing around, when she fell. Midair, she had the fleeting thought that someone had pulled the very pavement out from under her like a rug, but when she landed with a flat thud, her ankle twisted in an implausible angle, she knew that she'd slipped in the slimy rivulet that was making its way towards some distant sewer, a serpent that had been stalking and trailing them all along, waiting to strike, to pluck from the red-hatted herd the weakest among them. As she lay there on the grimy cobblestone, Howard and Bilal crouching near her, she saw how filthy the streets were, caught glimpses of feral cats dashing through the shadows, stared at the dirty feet of the people looking down on her. The bright colors and shiny objects were dimmed by the smells of unwashed bodies and baking trash. How did I miss all this before, she thought as she lay there, not yet realizing that she was crying, and was somehow comforted by the rottenness of the place; at least now, she thought, I am seeing things clearly.

❧

They'd taken her to the Dar al Fouad Hospital where she was treated by an Egyptian doctor with a British accent. She'd fractured her ankle in two places, and sprained her wrist and elbow trying to break her fall. Howard and Bilal had stayed with her the whole time, Howard performing the role of intrepid steward with obvious glee. She was given pain pills and crutches and relocated carefully back to her hotel room like a delicate piece of antique furniture. Howard sat on the edge of her bed and asked her if she wanted to go home. She'd said yes before he finished the question. The earliest flight

All That You Forgot to See

back to JFK was at three in the morning. Bilal alone had knocked on her door at midnight, packed up her toiletries and the few items hanging in the closet, and maneuvered her down into the waiting taxi. He rode in the front seat with the driver making easy conversation while Althea stared out the window, making their way back to the airport like a tape in rewind.

Back on her balcony, her leg propped up on a pillow, she sorted through the photos she'd taken of her two days in Egypt. She had no knack for it whatsoever. She might've just closed her eyes and held her camera away from her body, pressing the button at random; in fact, she recalled an exhibit at the Met where the artist had done precisely that, and called it art. She spread the images before her like clues to a puzzle. She'd snapped a cursory picture of the Nile while crossing one of the many bridges; now, she saw that she'd captured a group of teenage girls in neon pink and yellow, giggling and waving at a group of boys on the far bank. There was one of the canopied streets of Zemalek, lined with bookstores and coffee shops, where a woman in the foreground, walking towards her, was Althea's spitting image; her Egyptian doppelganger, in every way but clothing. In another shot, of the Al-Azhar Mosque courtyard, where the carpet was partitioned into rectangles for prayer, a toddler was proudly showing her parents a summersault while they beamed down at her; she'd been so uncomfortable in the mosque at the time, enduring their tour with her eyes half closed like she was making her way through a haunted house. She picked up a photo from behind the Pizza Hut window. Perhaps she'd accidentally turned on the flash, perhaps it was simply her angle in that moment, but in the center of the photo was a bright burst of light, yellow and white and blue. Behind it she could make out the shape of a pyramid — vague and out of focus — the blast of light at once a star, on second thought an angel, and then again fire.

All That You Forgot to See

The Authors

Tara Isabella Burton wrote "Lady in a Tower," which is fiction. Her essays, reviews, and travel writing can or shall be found at *National Geographic Traveller*, *Los Angeles Review of Books*, *Salon*, *Guernica*, *Conde Nast Traveller*, and many other places. Her fiction has appeared or is forthcoming in *Arc*, *Shimmer*, *[PANK]*, and more. She is the winner of *The Spectator*'s 2012 Shiva Naipaul Memorial Prize for travel writing and the author of the novel *A Thief in the Night*, which is currently on submission.

Kimberly Cawthon wrote "Cindy in Manhattan," which is fiction. She strives to love, be loved, and write it all down. She is a true southwestern girl and sunshine addict who grew up in the wide-open states of New Mexico and Arizona. She is a fiction writer, playwright and educator who recently earned an MFA in Creative Writing from Northern Arizona University. Her fiction has appeared in *Four Ties Lit Review*. She is also a reader for *Thin Air Magazine*. Her ten-minute play, *Egg Whites & Cantaloupe*, was recently performed by the Northern Arizona Playwriting Showcase. In the summer of 2013, she plans to complete her first novel, a work of interconnected short stories titled *Her Gold*. She also expects to make sun tea and work on her tan. She lives in Phoenix, Arizona.

Travis Dahlke wrote "Snail Honey," which is fiction. He is a freelance writer and illustrator from Connecticut. He is the author of *Children's Stories for Grown Ups*, which can be found floating around the Internet. He is a recent graduate of Eastern Connecticut State University, where he studied graphic design and creative writing.

Danusha Goska, PhD, a New Jersey teacher and writer, wrote "Our Unlikely Fusion," which is non-fiction. The child of Eastern European immigrants, she has lived and worked in Africa, Asia and Europe, as well as on both coasts and in the heartland of the United States. Her work has appeared in anthologies including *The Impossible Will Take a Little While* and *Folklore Muse*. Her memoir, *Save Send Delete*, tells the true story of a debate about God and a love affair she shared with a prominent atheist. *The Happy Catholic* blog named *Save Send Delete* one of the ten best books of the year. In April 2013, Goska was teaching William Paterson University.

Erika Jung wrote "Victor and Pamina," which is fiction. She is a recent graduate of Brown University, where she studied literary arts and psychology. She sees her two fields of interest as highly complementary, as both seek to understand human behavior through some form of narrative. Her work has appeared in *Elimae, Leonard's Mad Death, Heartbreaker, Construction, InDigest,* and *Our Stories.* In January 2012, *Urban Confustions* magazine featured Jung as "author of the month." After spending 2012 teaching English in Spain, she moved to Chicago to pursue a PhD in Clinical Psychology at Northwestern University.

Naima Lynch wrote "All That You Forgot to See," which is fiction. She has been writing stories for as long as she could hold a pen. She grew up in Monterey, California where she cultivated a love for morning fog, coffee shops, and paperback copies of Flannery O'Connor's short stories. As a grown-up, she has lived and worked throughout the Middle East, primarily in Yemen, Afghanistan and Dubai. It was in these vivid countries where she learned to seek the stillness at the heart of chaos — and to try to write about it.

She holds an MA in Middle Eastern Studies from the University of Chicago, and has written extensively on the politics and culture of the region. Before earning her

MA, she studied Anthropology and Religious Studies at the University of North Florida. In mid-2013, she was living in Sydney, Australia, where she was working on a series of Polaroid-inspired paintings, a collection of short stories, and an unruly spate of long naps.

Doreen E. Massey, who also writes as Elizabeth J. Hall, wrote "Upside Down Trees," which is fiction. She is a Labour peer with a special interest in children, young people and families. She is chair of the All Party Parliamentary Group for Children, a trustee of Unicef UK and a patron of many charities focused on women and children. She was previously a teacher who worked in London, Africa and the US, director of the young people's programme at the Health Education Council and chief executive of the Family Planning Association. She has worked as a consultant on health education in Central Asia and Russia. She is married with three children. Her interests include travel, reading, walking, Pilates and swimming. In April 2013, she was working on her first novel and continuing to write short stories.

Mohita Nagpal wrote "The Girl with the Egg-Shaped Face," which she says is seventy percent non-fiction, thirty percent fiction. Until the twelfth grade, she never thought of anything except becoming a professional athlete. She was a national roller hockey player and a decent volley player. However, the world isn't very kind to such dreams, especially for those who happen to be women. So she ended up becoming a journalist.

Mohita finished school and her undergraduate degree in Delhi, and then earned a post-graduate degree in journalism from the Asian College of Journalism in Chennai. In April 2013, she was working in the editorial department of the *Hindustan Times* newspaper, a job that eats up her weekends and evenings.

She likes to read Haruki Murakami, listen to the Beatles, watch Woody Allen movies and eat pasta. She is a horrible dancer and her teenage years were pretty much consumed with thinking up excuses for not attending parties. These days, she is teaching herself how to swim and meditate. She wants to write a novel some day, run a cozy little Italian eatery and spend a charmed life in a humble beach house. Of these three, only the first one is a permanent, unflinching desire. The other two change depending on her state of mind.

Catherine Onyemelukwe wrote "The Memorable Memo," which is non-fiction. She graduated from Mount Holyoke College in 1962 with a degree in German. She began her career as a Peace Corps Volunteer in Nigeria. She taught German to sixth-form (post-high school) students and English and African History at a secondary school. She met her husband during her second year in the country. The unusual wedding of a Peace Corps Volunteer and a host country national was picked up by international media, and *Life* magazine ran a photo. She learned her husband's native language, Ibo. During Nigeria's civil war (the Biafran War) she lived with her husband and two small children in his village for a year before leaving for Portugal and the US until the war's end in 1970.

She left teaching in 1977 to run her own fashion company. She returned to the US in 1986 to earn an MBA at Yale University. Her husband followed and has become an American citizen. She has worked for several nonprofits. She was a board member of the Peace Corps alumni association. She published an article describing her son's traditional marriage in Nigeria for the Friends of Nigeria newsletter in 2007. She was president of the board of the Westport Public Library in the 1990s and, later, president of the board of the Unitarian-Universalist United Nations Office (UU-UNO). She travels to Nigeria regularly.

Joanna Pocock wrote "The Road to Napanee," which is fiction. She is a Canadian writer living in London. In 2000, she graduated with an honors MA in Creative

Writing from Bath Spa University. She was recently longlisted for the Bath Short Story Award, for which the winners had not — in April 2013 — yet been announced. In 2012, she was shortlisted for *Mslexia*'s short story competition and the *Lightship International* first novel award. She won joint first prize in the 2010 Segora short story competition, which she went on to judge in 2011. She has had stories published in *Cooldog* and *Ritptide* magazines.

In mid-2013, she was working on her third novel and collaborating on a film about addiction. Since 1999, she has been teaching creative writing at Central St Martins in London, and has also taught at life writing at Bath Spa University and genre fiction at Roehampton University. When she isn't writing and teaching, Joanna works as a copy-editor for Verso Books, among other publishers.

Kathryn Shaver wrote "L'Amoureux," which is fiction. She spent two decades at the helm of the advertising agency she founded, then developed an international consulting practice for privately held companies in former Communist Bloc countries. After retiring from the business and civic community in 2003, she completed an MFA in Fiction from Spalding University. Her first published story was the 2008 Fiction Prize winner for *Inkwell Journal*, and she has garnered an honorable mention or been named a finalist in a dozen other competitions. Her stories have also appeared in *Narrative Magazine*, *Dos Passos Review*, *Persimmon Tree*, the *Louisville Courier-Journal* and several fiction anthologies. A Louisville, Kentucky native, she graduated from Auburn University with a degree in design, and continues to use her early design training in painting, portraiture, and fiber arts. An avid gardener, she divides her time between Louisville and Savannah, Georgia.

Nina Shengold wrote "April in Leningrad," which is fiction. Her books include the novel *Clearcut* (Anchor Books), *River of Words: Portraits of Hudson Valley Authors* (SUNY Press, with photographer Jennifer May), and twelve theatre anthologies edited with Eric Lane (Vintage Books, Viking Penguin). She won the Writers' Guild Award for her teleplay *Labor of Love*, starring Marcia Gay Harden. Shengold lives in New York's Catskill Mountains, where she is books editor at *Chronogram* magazine.